CODE NAME: SOUCOUYANT

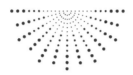

NORIAN LOVE

Copyright

© 2023 by Norian Love

© 2023 by Project 7even Publishing

ISBN-13: 978-1-7366707-8-1

ISBN-10: 1-7366707-8-6

For Mom
Love always

ACKNOWLEDGMENTS

Before we start, I'd like to thank each and every person who took the time to read this far into the series. I hope you are having as much fun as I am writing these stories. There are always so many people to thank when a project like this comes to life.

As always, I like to thank my team. The Project 7even family is growing (and I'm here for it)!

I'd like to thank my family and friends for all of their support but specifically, I'd like to shout out my mom.

Fun fact. My mom largely inspired this book. For as long as I could remember I was afraid of the Soucouyant, a West Indian boogeyman of sorts. This book is special to me because now as an adult, I get to share some of the culture that shaped me and also, as far as bad ass women go, in my eyes my mother will always be a super-hero. I've seen her do far more fantastic things than most of what you will read. I've never met anyone more brave, loving, or fearless. Thanks mom for everything.

Now some of you are gonna ask, wait, your mother was a spy? To which I'll promptly say no, (unless you count her superhuman ability to figure out what trouble I was even thinking about getting into.) but what she will always be is an amazingly constructed, beautifully complex woman with a heart of gold. Love you, ma mère.

Enjoy the book!

Great tribute!

Soucouyant *noun.* (ˌso͞oko͞oˈyäN) - A shapeshifting Caribbean folklore character who appears as a reclusive woman by day. By night, she strips off her skin and puts it in a mortar. In her true form, as a fireball she flies across the dark sky in search of a victim. Because of her shape shifting abilities, the Soucouyant can become anyone or anything. She can even enter the home of her victims through any sized hole like cracks, crevices and keyholes.

THE AGENCY

"*B*efore we start, I need you to be honest with me. How do you feel?"

Shanice thought back to the series of events leading up to this moment.

It was a great question.

In the past month she'd been drugged, drowned to death, brought back to life, and held prisoner, only to sign up to be potentially killed again as a member of the CIA.

She touched her ribs, still healing from her recent ordeal. It had been almost two months since the CIA had held her captive, her final qualifying test to assess her readiness to join the Agency.

A swarm of butterflies fluttered in her stomach as she walked down the hall with Director Caldwell. She scanned the hallways of the CIA headquarters, dozens of men and women all concealing various secrets. Soon she'd have secrets of her own to keep, and the thought excited her.

She looked at Caldwell. "Well, my friends think I'm dead. I think I'm a mixture of genuine excitement and, 'What the hell did I get myself into?'"

"Sounds about right. Okay, Agent Gibson, the doctor said you're cleared for active duty. Welcome to the Agency."

"Thank you, Director, it's an honor. About Sergeant Winters and Corporal Holt, I really would like—"

"We've gone over this, Agent Gibson. You're in the CIA now. You signed up to be a field agent. It can be a wonderful job, but if you're distracted, it will ultimately cost you your life out there. Keep your head in the game now. Worry about that when you get off assignment."

The two continued to walk. It wasn't the answer she wanted, but it was the one she decided to live with for now.

"So, since I'm an agent now, do I get a code name or what?"

Director Caldwell ignored her question. She wasn't sure if he'd heard her or not about the code name. She wasn't sure he cared, but she decided not to press the issue.

He was a good-looking man; middle-aged, half black, half Arabic, with light brown eyes. Shanice estimated him to be roughly six-foot-one, compared to her own height of five-foot-seven. His eyes told a story of fatigue. She imagined that was the price of years of secrets and deception.

The pair walked into a room labeled *Omicron*. In it were several workstations, all facing outwards. Several people were in the room working, though they promptly stopped once Caldwell sat at the black metal table in the middle of the large room. He ushered Shanice to sit in the chair to his right.

Director Caldwell pushed his glasses against his face and removed his kufi, exposing his curly salt-and-pepper hair. "Okay everyone, I'll keep this brief. This is Agent Shanice Gibson, code name Agent Zero. She's our newest field operative. She has worked with us in the past on loan, but now she's going to be a primary asset in the field. Agent Zero, meet Xavion Digs, lead analyst in our cyber security department."

"Xavion, you're the guy I've been training with online in cyber security?"

"It's finally good to put a body—I mean, a face with the name," Xavion flustered. "You can call me Professor X."

"I can, but I won't."

As Shanice smirked, Caldwell continued. "And I believe you've already met Agent Victor Reynolds."

"I don't think I'll ever forget him," Shanice mused as she looked at the man she'd come to know as Hal, who'd held her captive in her final test. He nodded in return, no hard feelings left between them.

She turned back to Caldwell. "So, about that code name. How did we decide on Zero?"

"Agent Zero, code names are earned in the field. For now, you are Agent Gibson – or internally, Agent Zero."

"Oh, like in James Bon—"

"No, Agent Zero. If you pay as little attention in the field as you are right now, there's a zero percent chance you're going to survive this mission."

His curt response squelched her childlike nervousness.

"I see this isn't the place for levity."

"Not at all. I can appreciate some soldiers may want to lighten the mood before a serious assignment, but as I said, this isn't the Army – this is the CIA. I'm currently the direct liaison for twenty-six operations worldwide. So no, I don't have time for levity, or anything not related to the mission. Now if we can get back to it, that would be most helpful. After all, it's your life on the line."

"Yes, sir, I understand."

"And we don't do formalities – actually, never mind. We don't have time for this. What do you know about the Seven Syndicate?"

"I'm familiar with the name. They're a hacktivist group, right?"

"They're much more than that. The Seven Syndicate is responsible for some of the biggest data hacks and terror attacks in the U.S. and around the world. Their leader, a man using the moniker Sandoval, is a strategic mastermind. We believe him to be of Latin descent, since their first act of terror was the destabilization of El Salvador's economy. Their economic downturn made him a billionaire, with his fortune hidden in Bitcoin.

"His plans so far are a mystery. What we do know is, for the past year, our counterintelligence surveillance team has been hearing whispers of an unverified event known only as 7-Up. We've been trying to learn more about their methods, but each time one of our assets gets close, they end up dead. And then yesterday, we received this."

Director Caldwell picked up the remote and pressed play. A man dressed in black appeared on the TV screen. His face was covered by a black mask with a blue '7' stitched in the center.

He began to speak in a deep, modulated voice. "Your time as a festering wound on civilization is nearing its end. The citizens of this society no longer believe the falsehoods you perpetrate, as a government here for our benefit. We've suffered in your wars while you fed off the blood, sweat, and tears of the poor. Enjoy your remaining days. The world is changing, and the old way of living is dying out. We are the Seven."

As the video ended, Caldwell pulled up another screen. "About six weeks ago, a notorious American hacker who goes by the screen name 'Hummingbird' posted on the dark web. She needed help building a game-changing program simply known as The Algorithm. Xavion was able to befriend her using a false profile he created, 'Starkiss'. The two worked on a piece of the Algorithm, but two days ago Hummingbird's behavior changed. She told Starkiss to stop working on the Algorithm, and then went dark. She sent Starkiss an encrypted message that read 'SS 7UP TI'."

"What does that mean?" Shanice asked

"We're not entirely sure, but our best guess is 'Seven Syndicate 7-Up Threat Imminent'. Hummingbird was supposed to resume working on the Algorithm twelve hours ago, but so far she's been silent."

Xavion turned to his computer, tapping his keyboard diligently. Within a few moments, his computer screen was projected at the front of the room. He walked up to the large screen. "So, me and Hummingbird, we're working on a relatively complex code sequence, just a small piece of what the Syndicate is calling The Algorithm.

From what we can tell, its primary function is math-related. Hummingbird was contracted to write it and brought me on when she fell behind the deadline. We wrote only about a few dozen lines of code for the project, so I took a risk and put a tracker in the software, but that's when everything went haywire. She disappeared after that."

⌐so yall fucked up and blew her cover?

"So, am I going in to extract her?" Shanice asked.

Caldwell chimed in. "We have to assume she's dead or compromised. Your job is to find out which one."

"Okay, and assuming I find her? Then what?"

"You won't," Xavion replied. He pointed to a document on the screen and continued. "From what I know about the Syndicate, the little I could find of them on the dark web, all work is segmented and assigned to pairs as a failsafe to keep them isolated. That means that, whatever they're working on, they still need my data to make it work. Hummingbird was last working from Italy, but counterintelligence found her final message originated in the West Indies. We're assuming whoever is behind this project is looking for a hacker in that region that they believe to be Starkiss, because I set my terminal to bounce from Turks and Caicos," Xavion said.

Caldwell walked to the center of the room. "We think whoever has Hummingbird is looking for Starkiss and is going there to find them. Whatever they're building, they need this data, and they'll stop at nothing to get it, because the Algorithm isn't complete without it."

Shanice nodded in agreement and asked, "So, what's the plan?"

"You will go undercover as Starkiss, aka Mari Patterson, the dark-web hacker who has been working with Hummingbird. Whoever is behind this needs the other hacker to finish the Algorithm."

"They're going to know I'm not a hacker the moment I open my mouth." *It is not going to work. Yall setting her up*

"You're not giving yourself enough credit. You know the difference between a VGA and an HDMI cable?"

"I never said I was an idiot," she scoffed jokingly.

"A big part of your deception will be confidence. You just need to look comfortable around technology, sit behind the keyboard like a hacker. Our training should help you a lot," Xavion smiled like a proud father.

Shanice rolled her eyes. It was true, their weeks of training in mid-level cyber security did indeed have some benefits.

He handed Shanice a USB flash drive. "I grilled you inside and out on the intricacies of our code. I built it, so I know it's solid. I'm also sure you'll be able to answer just about any reasonable question that might come up. But as a precaution, I finished the work early and even put a little code on the drive that will self-replicate or reboot to its default setting if there's any trouble. When they make contact, all you have to do is give them this Micro USB key and it will finish the job they need from Starkiss. You should be set. I've embedded code that will give me external control of your computer, and won't trigger any firewalls. We may not be able to see where they are or what they're doing, but we'll be able to make sure the Algorithm is running properly."

"Well, once they have the finished Algorithm, won't they just try to kill me?"

"We think they'll try to convert you," Caldwell said as he stood up again. "From what we know about the Seven Syndicate, they are smart, cunning, and ruthless. You'll need to be the same. We've got one shot at this, so we have to make it count.

"Alright, everyone, we know our assignments. Wheels up in thirty."

As the room broke up to move to their assignments, Shanice waited until Caldwell was alone before she approached him. "Thank you for recruiting me, sir. I won't let you down."

"I was actually against it, but you tested off the charts, and the last time we had an agent do as well as you did, he led to the capture of Osama Bin Laden. I was outvoted."

Shanice thought about his words as he walked out of the room. It was the opposite of what she needed to hear. She needed to know why he felt that way.

She ran to catch up to him. "Sir, respectfully, none of what you're saying makes sense. You're sending me into the field, but you have no confid—"

"Because, Agent Gibson – or should I say Agent Zero – your Army training is comparative to performing a medical procedure with a double-edged sword."

"Excuse me? Sir, you're an Army ranger. In fact, I don't understand what that has to do wi—"

"The world has changed, Agent Zero." He heaved a sigh before continuing. "There used to be a time that, when our enemies attacked, we knew exactly which country to turn into a parking lot. But now our foes are faceless, nameless, and smart. They're spread out all over the world, in coffee shops or college campuses, and they're growing in number every year. That's a harder target to kill; it's like carving out an infection, you need a scalpel for that. We need more scalpels, fewer swords."

Caldwell walked off as Shanice processed his words.

Agent Reynolds approached her. As she stood next to her former captor, she mused, "It feels weird to call you anything but Hal."

"Gonna be a lot of weird around here, Gibson. For example, I'm about to work with the woman that tried to kill me."

"Yeah, sorry, not sorry about that."

"We're square, just pointing out the weird."

Shanice nodded in acknowledgement.

"How are your ribs?" Reynolds asked.

"I won't be playing tackle football anytime soon, but I'll live. How's your thigh?"

"Well, what's left of it is healing up quite nicely. Should be back in the field in a couple weeks." There was a pause before Agent Reynolds continued. "Also, you can still call me Hal."

"Thanks Hal. So, what's Caldwell's story?"

Hal sighed. "Caldwell is the real deal. You know that credible threat the president ignored from a reliable source regarding 9/11?"

"Yeah?"

"He was the reliable source."

Shanice's eyes widened. She was suddenly seeing Caldwell with new eyes. "Wait. He was Raven Claw?"

"The one and only."

"I heard stories overseas about an agent that infiltrated Al Qaeda. Gave us a lot of actionable intel. Saved our lives a few times over. It's one thing to hear the stories, it's a totally different thing to meet the man."

"Don't worry, that reverence goes away real fast, then it comes back."

"I'm not following you."

"Caldwell was one of the Agency's best agents. He stayed under for ten years at one point, working multiple assignments, never breaking any of his covers. That fast-tracked him for the Middle East gig. America didn't have anyone in the region – sure, they had a few political allies and enemies in their pocket, but they couldn't get any intel in real time. Al Qaeda was well-insulated at that time. We needed a way in, and Malik Caldwell volunteered for the job."

"Taking that post made him a legend."

"Caldwell was embedded in an Al Qaeda cell a year before 9/11. He didn't do any decompression therapy from his previous assignments; he went straight into the belly of the beast. He worked his way up the ranks until he got to Osama himself. That's how we were able to take him out."

Shanice watched the man in question talking to other suits in the hallway.

In several military circles, Raven Claw was a legend. She personally had benefited from his actionable intelligence when she was in the military.

"I can't believe I'm working for the Raven Claw," she mumbled.

"When he came back home, half the Agency considered him a hero. The other half thought he was an Al Qaeda mole, but if you ask me, the man's a national treasure."

Shanice studied Caldwell with this new knowledge. She was in awe of him.

He caught her watching him and walked back towards the pair. "Maybe you didn't hear me the first time. I said wheels up in thirty."

2

ISLAND TINGZ

Turks and Caicos - three weeks later

"Coffee, Jamaican blend, two creams, two sugars," Shanice said to the barista behind the counter.

She'd been in Turks and Caicos for nearly a month, with no sign of Hummingbird or anyone even remotely associated with the Seven Syndicate. A part of her wondered if this was another initiation test. Still, she stayed the course.

Shanice had been scoping out the local cafés and restaurants, to no avail. She had no idea who she was supposed to be looking for. She'd never met Hummingbird, only knew she was a hacker, presumably in her mid-twenties.

And more importantly, she had no idea what Sandoval looked like. The Agency's best assessment of him was a Latino man born in central America. Since she'd been there, she'd been studying the Spanish men on the island, always on the lookout for him.

She decided to make her call to headquarters early. She dialed the pre-programmed number.

"I'm calling to check on an emerald necklace."

"Sure, do you have your receipt number?"

"Yes, it's Omicron 346."

"Your passcode is confirmed, Agent Zero. Another dry day, huh?"

"So far there's been no sighting of anybody matching the current description we have of Sandoval," she said into her wireless headphones.

"Stay patient, Zero. They'll come out in the open. They have to complete this device. Are you wearing the necklace?"

Shanice touched the necklace in question, a gold pendant shaped like a star, a pair of lips engraved in the middle. "I am."

"Then they'll make contact. Have patience."

"Patience has never been my virtue. Look, all I see is the ocean water, overweight, middle-aged men, and locals. No sinister plot. Who even plots on a tropical island, anyway? I thought these things were hatched in underground lairs or something."

Xavion laughed. It felt good to talk to someone who wasn't as strict as Caldwell or as cold as Hal. Xavion was a geek, but also loved muscle cars and boats, some of the same things she enjoyed.

It also felt good to be on the island. She hadn't spent much time in the West Indies since she was a child. She wanted to go swimming, since there was nothing to do but wait.

"Xavion, let me ask you. Will you tell Caldwell if I get out of here early? No one is coming. This is a pointless endeavor. I might as well make the most of my time here."

"I agree. The truth is, if Sandoval is as careful as we think he is, you won't need to find him – he'll find you."

"That's what I think, but it's been two weeks of nothing. Are you sure this necklace is enough bait? Because right now all I have is crickets."

"It has to be; anything more obvious will probably spook them."

"Okay, well, if you don't hear from me again, I've either died by the Syndicate hands or boredom. I'm out."

Shanice hung up the phone. She put her belongings in her bag and decided to get another coffee to go. As she got to the counter, a handsome, dark-skinned man with shoulder-length dreadlocks reached the spot at the same time and ushered the barista over.

"Excuse me, miss, I'd like to get the gentleman sitting in the corner a double expresso with one cream. And to apologize for pushing in, I'd like to pay for this lady's coffee too."

"Oh, thanks," Shanice replied.

"My pleasure."

She examined him. His British accent was light but noticeable. His powder-blue linen shirt clung to his chiseled chest and fell flat against his rock-hard abdomen. His smile was alluring, to say the least.

The barista handed her the coffee, and Shanice turned to the man. "You didn't have to do that, but thank you."

"It's my pleasure. I haven't seen you around before. Are you here on vacation?"

"Yeah, just spending some quality time reading. But I'm done for the day."

The man accompanied her as she headed toward the door, stopping to grab a few napkins.

"So, what are you reading?"

"I just started a book called *Not a Chance*."

"Oh, really? What's it about?"

"It's about a girl trying to mind her own business, when she's approached by a guy who buys her a cup of coffee, not realizing that he doesn't have a shot with her."

The man chuckled. "Well, since you're at the beginning of the book, maybe the guy gets a shot in the end? Maybe they have a spot of tea together."

"Doubtful, but it's cute that he thinks so."

The man chuckled again and extended his hand. "Hi, my name is—"

"We're done here."

"But I—"

"I said, we're done."

Without another word, Shanice left a tip for the barista and walked away. The man returned to his table.

that was Sandoval! Lol

He was very attractive, but she had no interest in being a local's one-night-stand.

It's been three weeks. Maybe our intel was wrong.

She decided she'd go to the beach and relax for the day.

Spending her days at various restaurants and coffee shops, and her nights at local clubs, she'd become familiar with the area and its people, but she was no closer to her target.

As she turned the corner, she noticed something different about her surroundings. There were several unfamiliar faces in the immediate vicinity, people who hadn't been there in the past three weeks, standing in multiple groups.

Something's wrong.

She spotted a couple, having what appeared to be a normal conversation.

Next, a slender man jogging, wearing a hoodie in 85° weather. white people!

She peered back at the couple. Both of them were wearing hoodies.

She pulled out her phone and took a selfie, ensuring to capture the couple in the background. She examined the photo. Her instincts were screaming at her.

It's a trap.

Shanice deleted the photo. The man who was jogging turned around and ran in her direction as she resumed walking.

She knew she was about to be abducted.

She unlocked her phone and called base as she walked quickly, gaining distance between her and her would-be captors.

"Omicron, I think I've just made contact. Wipe my phone," she ordered.

Shanice quickly hung up the phone and put it back in her purse. The team would need time to erase the phone data.

Instead of taking her normal path, she darted into a nearby restaurant and hurried into the kitchen. She peered back, only to spot the jogging man entering the restaurant, closely followed by the couple.

She looked at her phone. Her call logs to the Agency were being erased and replaced with local phone numbers. The process was only 52% complete.

She scrambled out of the kitchen and out the back entrance, rushing down the alleyway while peeking at her phone again.

71%.

"Damn it," she spat.

She was running out of time and her captors were closing in. Though she knew she could take them in hand-to-hand combat, any resistance would blow her cover.

She hurried into a local store full of tropical dresses and moved past the owner. She looked at her phone again.

93%.

She snatched one of the dresses and ran out of the back door. The owner yelled as she sprinted out the back door, only to run into a solid wall.

Straightening, she looked up and locked eyes with the burly six-foot-five, mocha-toned man she met in the coffee shop.

He stood blocking her path.

She tried to turn around and run, but instantly felt an electric sensation of a taser.

She passed out instantly.

3

THE SEVEN SYNDICATE

"*R*ise and shine."

A grizzly voice brought Shanice back to consciousness.

Her eyes were heavy, the pain from the taser amplifying her still-healing ribs. She scanned the room and saw the large man who tased her and several unfamiliar faces working at computer terminals in a nearby room.

This is the syndicate. Show time.

She feigned fear as she asked, "Where am I? Wh—who are you?" She added a body tremble to sell it further.

Suddenly, a familiar voice spoke. "You dropped your cup of coffee, so I got you another one. Two creams, two sugars, right?"

That accent.

She turned to the voice. It belonged to the same handsome, dark-skinned man she'd met in the coffee shop.

"Who are you?"

"We'll get to that," the man promised.

Shanice tried to move but couldn't. They'd tied her to the metal chair.

"Look, I hate to break it to you, but women don't like being tased on their first date. If this is how you handle rejection…"

The man chuckled. "I'm sorry about that bit of unpleasantness. But we have to be careful."

"Listen, if you're thinking about trafficking me, I have family and—"

"No, you don't, Mari Patterson – or do you prefer your screen name, Starkiss?"

Shanice grew quiet.

This was definitely the Seven Syndicate.

She looked at the man and asked again. "Who are you?"

He ignored her question. "You dropped out of MIT after two semesters and began stealing from millionaires to survive. It's a very admirable hustle."

She tried to loosen her bindings, the metal chair scraping against the concrete floor.

"Where am I?"

"You're home… at least for the next few months." He nodded to a larger man who pulled out a knife and walked over to the chair. He sliced through the ropes holding her captive.

Shanice rubbed her bruised wrists.

"To answer your earlier question, I am Adonis Carter. You would have known that had you been more pleasant earlier. Mr. B and I work for the Seven Syndicate." He motioned to the other man. "You can call him Bear."

Her eyes widened.

She'd been working off intel that said he was Spanish, but there was no trace of Latino in him. "You're Sandoval."

"I've been called that, and others. You look surprised."

"Well, with a name like Sandoval, you kinda expect a little less… melanin."

Sandoval laughed. "You're funny, you know that?"

"Where's Hummingbird?"

"She's no longer your concern."

"Did you kill her? Are you gonna kill me now to clean up the loose ends?"

Sandoval smirked and circled the chair. "Mari, if I wanted you dead, we wouldn't be having this conversation."

"Then why am I here?"

"The Algorithm. It's why we're all here. I want you to finish the job you started."

"How do I know you won't kill me once I'm done with the work?"

"I guess you don't have any guarantee, except my word and the hefty paycheck I'm offering, half of which I just deposited into your account."

Sandoval looked to the other man, who walked over to Shanice and handed back her phone. Shanice logged in to the bank app where the money would be.

US$10,000,000.

"Are you satisfied?"

She nodded. "And there's another ten million once I complete my part of the Algorithm?"

"There is. For now, let's walk."

Shanice stood up and the pair walked out of the dimly lit room.

On the other side of the door, the floral beauty of the tropical island was overwhelming. Her home for the next few months looked to be an idyllic villa set on the edge of the island.

Her nostrils filled with the scent of the ocean as the sun kissed her dark skin.

"Listen, Mari, I'm sorry about the way things were handled. I mean you no harm."

"You got a funny way of showing it."

"I guess I deserve that. I understand why you feel that way, but I hope you understand that these are dangerous times. Precautions are necessary."

Shanice nodded in agreement as the pair reached a balcony overlooking the ocean.

"So, if you don't mind me asking, what's all this for, anyway?"

"That's a complicated question. Maybe we can discuss it over dinner?"

"That's very flattering, but I already have dinner plans, and I'd like to keep them."

"Well, that's unfortunate, because you won't be able to make those plans."

Shanice peeked at him as he overlooked the balcony. As subtle as the threat was, it was clear: she wouldn't be leaving anytime soon.

She looked back at the ocean. "So, am I a prisoner?"

"Like I said, you are home. Consider yourself a valued guest. You're free to walk around the villa, but the only way anybody leaves is with me or one of my men."

"What about my clothing, all my stuff?"

"Anything you need, we will provide. In fact, there's a wonderful dress waiting for you in your suite. Your necklace is hanging from the bedroom door I've assigned to you."

Shanice touched her neck and realized that her necklace was missing.

He'd taken the bait.

"That's how you knew I was Starkiss."

Sandoval winked at her. "Shower and rest. Dinner is at 8."

4

SANDOVAL

*S*hanice looked at the time: 7:35.

She was almost ready for dinner. She looked at the dress – a black, elegant form-fitting dress – and smiled. Whether he was a terrorist or not was yet to be determined, but he definitely was a charming man.

She tried on the dress, fitting almost too perfectly.

Was this dress tailored?

She dismissed the idea and opened the remaining box, revealing a pair of red open-toed heels, also her size. The last box contained a red purse with a gold buckle. A single bottle of perfume had been left on the bedside table.

"Creed Aventus for women?" She sprayed the perfume and instantly fell in love. "This shit smells like heaven!" she said aloud. She felt sexy and beautiful, a rarity for her, since she owned only two dresses in her real life.

She thought back to her previous assignments when she was undercover in the Army. None of them involved tropical islands and handsome men. But the CIA wasn't the Army, she had to continually remind herself.

Sandoval was charming, but he was also the target. She couldn't take him down until she knew more about what he was doing.

It was important to send a message to Omicron to let them know she'd made contact. She couldn't trust that Sandoval hadn't bugged her phone to monitor all her activity. She had to assume it was compromised. She'd need to find another way.

As she finished getting dressed, there was a knock at the door.

Bear stood in front of her, arms folded. Shanice could tell by his expression he was caught off-guard by her appearance, but not as a man who was attracted to her.

She pressed the issue. "What's wrong, Bear? You look like you've seen a ghost."

He ignored her question. "Sandoval will see you now."

She nodded in agreement and picked up her phone, putting it in her new purse.

As they walked the compound, she counted the guards and assessed weak points in their defensive positions in case she needed to escape. She needed to get back to town soon to send Omicron a message. She also needed to locate Hummingbird, but her immediate concern was contacting base.

As they walked down the hall, Bear was silent, sneaking glances at her.

"Seriously, Bear, I don't know you, so if I'm walking into some weird orgy, I'm not—"

"What? No, it's nothing like that. It's just…"

"Just what?"

"You look just like her. Sandoval is in there," Bear said, now embarrassed by Shanice's comment.

He opened the large, oak double doors for her. On the other side of them, Sandoval stood in a black linen suit that exposed his bare chest right to his abdomen.

He was drinking a cognac in the softly-lit room, as the sound of waves crashing provided a natural ambiance, accompanied by the soft sound of Sade's Cherish the Day playing softly through a speaker.

She observed how the candles cast dancing shadows on the sand-colored walls. The marble floors were polished and immaculate, made to match the color of the walls.

As he turned around, his eyes widened, reminiscent of the look Bear had given when he'd first seen her.

Sandoval placed the glass on a table and walked over to her. "You look even more breathtaking than you did this morning."

"In my defense, they did electrocute me this morning."

"And now you're just electric."

She laughed at his unexpected response. He was clever, indeed.

He walked over to the table and pulled out a chair, motioning for her to sit. When she sat down, he scooted her to the table and walked around to sit in his own chair.

"Do you like the dress?"

"It's beautiful – fits better than anything in my closet. So do the shoes."

"Well, we should always make a beautiful woman feel as such. I'm happy I achieved my goal."

"I have to ask, how did you know my measurements?"

"To be honest, I got your measurements while you were being sent here. Like I said earlier, you'll be here for a while, so it was important for my tailors to know."

Shanice nodded. She didn't want to press the issue. She knew she had to toe the line against a man this calculated. She approached from another angle to test his limit. "Thing is, I wasn't prepared to stay, and I—"

"That's the end of the discussion, Mari. Now, I assure you, I will provide whatever you need. I know that's a hard thing to accept for someone who's used to taking care of themself, which I presume you are, but if you'll allow me, I promise I won't let you down."

His charm was undeniable. She knew very little about Sandoval, but she did know he meant every word.

She nodded and sipped the water that was sitting at the table. There was a stillness in the air.

"Did you like the perfume?"

"It's alright."

In fact, it was amazing, but she needed to pout a little to keep up the act of reluctant houseguest.

"That one is Baccarat Rouge 540. I picked it up in town today."

"I've never heard of it."

"I picked it up myself after we met."

"You mean, while I was running for my life from your goons?"

"That's the thing we're going to work on, Mari – perspective. I can appreciate why you felt you were in danger, but here we are having a candlelit dinner. With any luck, we can put all that unpleasantness behind us and have a good time."

"I'm sorry, it's just hard to get comfortable after the – what did you call it, unpleasantness? – with a man I know nothing about."

"You want to know something about me? Go ahead, ask away," he said as two waiters entered the room. Shanice watched as the plates were placed in front of her and Sandoval, loaded with locally-sourced seafood and a variety of sides. "Tell you what, I'll answer three questions, but for every questions I answer, you're gonna have to answer one. Oh, and enjoying yourself is nonnegotiable."

Shanice chuckled. "Deal."

"What's your first question?"

"Why the name Sandoval?"

"To keep it real? I have a lot of enemies, and people inherently stereotype. With a name like Sandoval, people are looking for a *True dat!* Spanish drug lord, and overlook the black guy from London. By then it's too late."

Shanice nodded. His strategy impressed her. After all, the CIA had done just that.

But the fact that she was still breathing was proof he hadn't caught on to her.

"What's your next question?" he insisted.

Shanice took a sip of the red wine sitting next to her grilled kingfish.

"Earlier, when Bear came to get me, he said, and I quote, 'you look just like her'. Who was he referring to?"

21

Sandoval took a sip of his Hennessey White. "You look like my mum… my mother, Angela Carter."

He took another sip of his drink as she processed his words.

He pulled out his phone and showed her a picture of him with a woman. Shanice could have been looking in a mirror, the resemblance was so striking.

"She's no longer with us, though I think she'd approve of Bear's assessment. You're both strikingly beautiful women," he said.

"I'm sorry for your loss. How long ago was it?"

"I was twelve. And with that, you've run out of questions."

"What? No, that didn't count."

"Rules are rules. I'm sorry. It's my turn now."

"Fine, go ahead with your stupid little questions," she joked as she sipped more wine. She realized she was starting to enjoy herself.

Sandoval took a sip of his whiskey and then asked, "So, Mari, do you have a boyfriend?"

"Oh, that's weak," she mocked.

Sandoval raised his hands in the air in surrender. "What?"

"Of all the questions…"

"It's what I want to know."

The pair laughed. He wasn't at all what she expected.

She took another sip of wine and replied. "I don't, but this is starting to feel like an audition."

"Perhaps it is."

His candor caught her off guard. "You don't even know me. Why?"

"I'm a man who knows what he wants. And right now, I want to get to know you." *You want a girl who looks like your mother?*

"No, I mean, why am I here? You want me to work on the Algo- *ohno* rithm, yet you haven't once asked me for the—"

"We found your USB drive when we raided your home. The component of the Algorithm you gave me has already been checked and is working the way I need it to. If it didn't, the last thing you would've seen was Bear when you were tased."

It impressed Shanice how thorough the Syndicate was.

She raised her eyebrows, and Sandoval, noticing the reaction, responded. "Like I said, I like to be a few steps ahead."

Shanice always knew that when going into the field, nothing in her home could expose her identity, so she wasn't worried about her cover being blown. She was more impressed by how efficient Sandoval and his men were. "So, you broken into my place, stole my USB key, and are already using my code. Why am I still here?"

"Your code is part of a much larger, more complex mechanism."

"You mean the Algorithm."

"It's a game changer, Mari. But I can't let you go anywhere until we know it works, and that's going to take months. I hope that $20 million you'll be receiving is more than enough to compensate for any work you lose out on during your time here. Plus, you get to stay on this tropical island. It's my hope that we can get better acquainted."

"And what—"

"If I'm not mistaken, that's three more questions. It's my turn to ask a question."

She heaved a sigh. "Fair enough. What's your question?"

"I'll ask you tomorrow at breakfast."

5

FIREBALL

3 a.m. Now or never.

Shanice knew she was being monitored, but wasn't sure exactly how. It was critical that she contacted Omicron.

She put on black tights and the darkest shirt provided to her and stepped outside. Security was still on patrol. Based on her recon earlier this evening, there was a five minute lull in between shift change when the area would be clear.

Gonna have to move quick.

There was a camera covering the main entrance, but a guard in the blind spot. She could get over the concrete wall if she had time, but the guard rarely moved from his location. She was more concerned with the masks they were wearing.

Every person on the compound was required to wear a black fencing mask with a '7' on them. She'd had one delivered to her room but hadn't needed it yet.

The mask has to have a viewing screen or something.

She couldn't worry about that yet. She had to find a way out.

She needed a distraction.

A car was idling in the circular driveway, waiting to be let in. Several of the cleaning crew stood just inside the gate waiting to be picked up. The guard moved to let the car in.

Shanice sprinted towards the edge of the villa, careful to avoid the cameras. She used a knoll at the edge of the compound to leap onto the wall and drop to the other side. The terrain on the other side was completely flat – her escape route was a one-way trip; she'd have to find another way back in.

"One problem at a time," she murmured.

For now, she needed to figure out where she was and how to get in touch with Omicron.

She jogged along the dimly-lit street, keeping her head down. After what felt like twenty minutes, the street met with the main road. She'd scouted the island when she first got here, and she estimated she was on the south side of the island.

I need to find a store.

People were lingering outside a dance club. She couldn't take the chance they were working for the Syndicate. Her best option was to steal a car.

She scanned the street for an older car; a security alarm would bring too much attention her way.

There was a turquoise '64 Cadillac Eldorado with a white interior about ten yards in front of her – and the top was down. She crept over and opened the door, keeping her head down.

It had been years since she'd worked in the auto shop, but some things you never forget.

Within minutes, she had the car started. Leaving the lights off, she slowly backed out of the parking spot and drove away from the main streets.

After a few minutes, she pulled over to revise her plan.

On the passenger seat sat a red baseball cap and a gray hoodie. She placed the ball cap over her plaited hair and slid the hoodie on before rummaging through the glove compartment. Buried under old papers and receipts were five $20 bills in U.S. currency.

She got back on the road, finding a store on the other side of the island roughly twenty minutes away that was still open. She walked

The whole Island probably belongs to them

into the store and paid for gas, a prepaid phone, a lighter, and a ten gallon gas can.

She turned on the prepaid phone and called Omicron.

"Floyd's Bakery, how may I help you?"

"Yes, I have a very important cake order due for delivery tomorrow. There have been some issues on our end, so I wanted to delay the delivery."

"That's fine. When would you like to reschedule the delivery for?"

"Unconfirmed at the moment, but it could be quite late. The host has some big changes in mind, and I haven't found the right decorations yet."

"Okay, keep looking. We'll make a note for the manager when he gets in. Thank you for calling, have great day."

Shanice hung up.

Her code indicated that everything was okay, but she hadn't made contact with Hummingbird yet. That would suffice.

She broke the phone in half and slid it down a nearby storm drain. She was just about to get back in the vehicle when a raised voice made her turn her head.

There was a woman walking by in a uniform. A man standing nearby had called to get her attention, but the woman either had earbuds in and hadn't heard him, or she was ignoring him.

He waited until she was in reaching distance to grab her and try to kiss her, the woman putting up a good fight. He was clearly intoxicated, and she wanted nothing to do with him.

Focus on the mission.

Shanice turned to the car to get in when she heard the woman scream. She looked over, but by then it was too late. The man had slapped the woman, and she'd fallen on the ground.

Shit!

She closed the door and walked over to where the woman was slowly getting up. The middle-aged drunk was standing over her, yelling with a slight Russian accent, as Shanice walked over towards the pair.

"Hey, asshole, you put your hands on her again and it'll be the last time you're able to use them without any pain."

The six-foot-one man turned around and sized her up. "What did you say to me?"

She stepped closer and replied, "I said, if you put your stank ass, pastrami-eating, vodka-drinking hands on her again, I'm going to fuck you up."

The Russian laughed. She could smell the stench of vodka on his breath. "I'd like to see you try, little bird."

"Well, come on, big papa. You ain't said nothing but a thing."

The man swung at Shanice, wildly missing.

She chuckled as she dodged, taunting him. "Is that all you got, papa? Thought you were going to show me something?"

The man swung again, this time with more precision, but he was too sluggish. Shanice ducked his swing and countered with a knee to the abdomen. *why?, Ya are showing them ya can fight*

The man grabbed her around the waist, amplifying the pain in her still-healing ribs. She moaned in agony.

"That's right, little bird, sing!" the man said as he compressed her ribs.

She swiftly raised her elbow in the air to deliver a violet strike to the side of the man's skull, forcing him to the ground.

She used her foot to force him to roll over. "Which hand is your writing hand?"

"What?"

She kicked the man in the eardrum. "There, now that your ears are unclogged, which hand is your writing hand?"

"My right!" the man moaned in agony.

Shanice walked to his side and stomped on his right hand repeatedly, until all his fingers were broken. "Learn to write with your left," she said.

A gasp had Shanice turning around to face the woman still on the ground, unharmed. "Are you okay?"

"*Si*," she replied.

Shanice turned and reached into the man's pocket, removing the money from his wallet.

"Here's a thousand dollars. Treat yourself."

The woman's mouth fell to the floor as she watched Shanice walk away.

Shanice was headed back to the car when she spotted a rock, the perfect size to be concealed by her fist. *This could be useful.*

When she got back to the car, she tossed the rock inside and look at the time: 4:15.

Shit.

She'd been gone over an hour, and the sun would lift some of the darkness soon. She had one last stop to make.

Shanice drove to a nearby CIA drop spot, where she knew a 9mm pistol waited for her. From there, she sped back to the villa and parked on an upward slope near the side of the estate.

She climbed on top of the car to ensure she could reach the wall and jump over. It was the perfect height.

Shanice reached for the pistol and sat it on the wall to secure it. She took off the hoodie and ball cap, noticing her necklace was missing.

Damn, I must have lost it in the fight.

She put the ball cap in the car and grabbed the gasoline, dousing the hoodie. Once it was decently saturated, she threw it on top of the wall. She put the car in neutral before taking the brick she'd picked up earlier and putting it on the brake pedal.

That won't last long. Gotta hustle.

She took the rest of the gas and poured it over the inside of the car and the convertible top. She tossed the can in the back of the car.

She climbed the car again and jumped to climb the wall. Lying flat, she grabbed the hoodie, lit it with the lighter and waited for the brick to lose its fight against the lever.

"Come on," she muttered. The car was still in neutral and the hoodie was catching fire to the point where it was too hot to hold on to. She was about to rethink her plan when the car began rolling.

"Finally," she breathed as she dropped the hoodie on top of the convertible hood, which instantly caught aflame. As the car gained momentum, the flames consumed the interior.

When the car made it to the edge of the road, it exploded, triggering the guards of the villa to run to the front gate.

Shanice grabbed the gun and waited until the coast was clear. Thankfully it was still dark enough to run to her room without being spotted.

Once inside her room, she locked the door and immediately found a hiding spot for the pistol. She then took off her clothes and took a shower to remove the smell of gasoline. The only change of clothes available to her had been supplied by Sandoval, delivered the night before while they were at dinner. She scented herself with the bottle of perfume.

She was about to lie down when there was a knock at the door.

She opened it, revealing Bear on the other side. "Sandoval needs to see you immediately."

6

JUST A KID WITH A BRICK

"Move it," Bear barked as he not-so-gently nudged Shanice forward.

"Ouch, you don't have to be an asshole, Bear," Shanice said as they walked to the main living quarters of the villa.

When they arrived, Bear opened the doors and Shanice was once again impressed by the breathtaking open concept. The wind lightly floated through the two-inch thick wood blinds. Sunlight would flow through the room as the day arrived.

Sandoval, sitting at a workstation with a state-of-the-art laptop connected to six monitors, stopped typing and stood. "What's going on, Bear?"

Shanice interjected. "I can answer that. Bear's being a bitch."

"Shut up and get in the room," Bear fired back.

She walked into the main hallway of the villa as Sandoval's phone shrilled.

He raised his finger to excuse himself while Shanice waited there.

She wasn't sure if Bear had spotted her escape – or even worse, if his men were currently searching her room. Still, her nerves of steel never wavered. This was the assignment.

After a moment, Sandoval got off the phone. "That was the prime minister. I assured him that we had nothing to do with that explosion earlier. Apparently, some drunk bloke was messing around on a lass, and the police think she burned his car to bloody hell."

"I disagree, mate," Bear rebutted.

Sandoval looked puzzled as he sipped his tea. "Well, speak your mind. I don't have all bloody day. The sun isn't even up yet. Why have you brought Mari here?"

Bear pushed her in front of him.

Sandoval immediately rebuked him. "Bear, I'm only going to say this once: never do that again. We respect our guests; we don't mistreat them."

Bear lifted both hands in surrender, pleading his case. "Adonis, listen to me. When I ordered the men to the front of the villa, I noticed someone running in the direction of her room. When I went to her room, she was inside."

Sandoval looked puzzled. "Right, because – and there's no other way to say this – it's her room. She should be inside."

"No, I mean, she wasn't there when I checked earlier."

"Why did you check earlier?"

"That's not the point. Where was she, Adonis?"

Sandoval looked to Shanice. "Well, he does bring up an interesting point. Where were you?"

"Not that it's any of your business, but I left my room to go for a jog around the villa. Since I value my privacy – unlike everyone here – I ran near the edge of the property."

"Even if it that were true, one of the men would've seen her. Why was she gone for so long?"

"Well, Bear, I lost my necklace, so like any normal person, I started looking for it. When I heard that explosion, it scared the shit out of me, so I ran back to my room. The reason I didn't answer the door was because I was shaken. If you'd like more details, I used your double-ply toilet paper, and I made sure I wiped—"

"That's enough," Sandoval interrupted, cutting off Shanice's sarcastic reply. He looked at his enforcer. "Bear, she was clearly jogging."

"It's not true, Adonis, I know what I saw. She wasn't running like she was scared; she was running low to the ground, like she was avoiding detection."

Shanice raised her hand. "Excuse me, no disrespect Mr. Bear, but you're, what, 6'7, 6'8? Do you even have any idea what low to the ground means?"

"An excellent point," Sandoval snickered.

"Furthermore, I'm sure this whole situation is probably normal for you, but being surrounded by gun-toting men wearing masks when I should be lying on the beach, might make the average person a little jumpy. I'm not used to explosions, so when I hear them in a place crawling with men armed to the teeth, my instinct is to run as low and fast as possible to the safest place, which was my room. This is feeling very Squid Game to me."

Bear ignored her entirely plausible explanation. "I don't care what she says. She was up to something. Hell, she may have even caused the explosion."

"With what? My good looks? Since you have all the answers, Bear, why don't you riddle me this? Why in the hell would I be trying to leave when I have twenty million reasons to stay?"

Sandoval weighed their words and, after a spell, asked, "Did you ever find your necklace?"

"I didn't."

"Then the answer is simple. I'll have my men search for your necklace, and if we find it, that's the end of the discussion."

"I don't know where it could be."

"Well, the good news is, if it's on this compound, we'll find it. Don't worry, we have metal detectors. I'll have the men begin looking immediately. Also, alert the groundskeepers; maybe one of them have seen it."

"You don't have to do that."

"No, I absolutely have to do that, Mari, because if you're lying, I won't have any other choice but to kill you. It's best we cross this bridge of trust and its penalty now."

Shanice nodded.

She knew the necklace was probably off the property. She needed to get back to her room to get her weapon. "Well, you do that, and I'll just go back to my room."

"Unfortunately, I can't let you do that. Besides, we're supposed to be having breakfast together this morning, and there's no time like the present. In fact, let's go have it on the beach. But first, let me put the call out to the groundskeepers and the guards to find this necklace."

Sandoval got on the walkie talkie and described the necklace, instructing his team to locate it. It was only a matter of time before they confirmed the necklace wasn't on the property. She needed to get back to her room.

"Is it okay if I go freshen up?"

"You look absolutely radiant as you are. No, we'll go have breakfast on the beach. Come with me – Chef Rein makes an excellent omelet."

She was headed to the patio when there was a buzz on one of the walkie talkies.

"Well, looks like there's been a development in case of the missing necklace," Sandoval announced. He got back on the walkie talkie and ordered the person to come into his chamber.

Hanging up, he moved to a hidden closet and pulled out a black mask and coat.

Shanice was stunned. His mask was different to the others; a slight silver lining lay along the edge of the mask.

Shit was about to hit the fan; she knew the necklace wouldn't be found. She could take Bear without a weapon, but she wouldn't be able to fight off Sandoval before the guards came.

She positioned herself near a window. It was a long drop to where the compound sat on the hill.

When the doors opened, her heart skipped a beat. One of the groundskeepers came in wearing a regular '7' mask. It was a woman – and she was holding the necklace.

"Everyone, this is Worker 9. She says she found your necklace."

The Spanish woman Shanice had defended earlier that night opened her hand and, sure enough, it was the Starkiss necklace she had been wearing.

Sandoval walked over and took the necklace while Bear questioned the lady. "Did you find this on our property?"

"*Si, Señor*. It was on the ground on the property."

"Was it near the edge?" Bear asked inquisitively.

"*No, Señor*, it was near the pretty flowers."

Sandoval walked over to Shanice and the necklace to her before turning back to the woman. "Thank you. You're free to go."

The woman nodded and quickly glanced at Shanice, both acknowledging the favor each had done for the other.

After a spell, Sandoval said, "Bear, you are free to go."

"But Adonis—"

"Leave us."

Bear nodded and glanced at Shanice as he walked out.

"Listen, I don't know what your friend has against me, but he's got—"

"I apologize for his behavior. Bear's just protective."

"Why?"

"So, we're asking questions again? Remember, it's my turn."

"I mean, technically, when you asked me if I'd found my necklace, that counted as one."

Sandoval laughed. "You are something else, aren't you? Well played."

"I'm just saying, if we're sticking to the rules, it's my turn."

Sandoval nodded and sighed. "I met Bear in a homeless shelter. He was already at least six-foot-two, weighing two twenty pounds, and only thirteen years old. Too big to feed or clothe, so he ended up at the shelter, same as all of us that the world forgot. Bear's problem was that some people would treat him like a man when he was just a boy. He was a gentle spirit.

"One day, I had just arrived at the shelter and Ken Burns – I'll never forget the name, he went by Tariq X back then – said he was a part of the nation of Islam but he was hiding out in London from all this rubbish he had supposedly done back in the States. In truth, he was a con artist and a bully, and Bear was his number one target."

Sandoval took a moment to process the painful memory. He

looked away as he continued. "So, this guy was pushing and shoving Bear, who wouldn't fight back, and then took his food. Bear hadn't eaten in three days. I didn't want to get involved – there were strict rules at the shelter – but he kept pushing Bear until he broke, and curled up in the corner crying.

"That wasn't enough for Ken. He started kicking the kid. No one helped him, and you gotta remember, he's just thirteen. I don't care how big he looks; that's a child he's kicking. I was undersized for being twelve years old at the time, but I'd never been soft. I grabbed a couple bricks, ran up to Tariq and clocked him in his eye.

"I had another brick ready to unload on the next guy, but I wasn't fast enough. He tackled me and snatched the brick out of my hand. He was about to split my skull open when the giant wallflower turned into a grizzly bear – that's how he got the nickname. He flung the dude halfway across the room. By this time some orderlies were coming, but Bear was in full beast mode. I had to talk him down and, when I did, they kicked us out. It's been the two of us ever since."

As Sandoval tried to contain his emotion, she walked over and sat next to him.

She understood the dynamics between an outcast and a friend coming to his rescue. She had a similar bond with Marcus. The man she'd loved her whole life. The one she'd left at home to die so she could be in this room.

"Mari, are you okay?"

She wasn't. She was worried about her own friend. He needed her help, and she was powerless.

Focus on the mission.

Caldwell's words echoed in her head.

She turned to Sandoval. "I'm fine. It's just sad that you guys met in a homeless shelter. I assume this was after your parents died?"

"I will tell you about that, but now's not the time. In fact, let's forget about all this unpleasantness and have that breakfast I promised you."

"Great. With your permission, I'd like to go freshen up. If that's okay with you, Mr. Sandoval, sir."

He snickered at her sarcasm. "Now that you know my real name, you could use it."

"What, Adonis?"

"Something wrong with Adonis?"

"A man named Adonis seems the type a woman would throw her panties at, and since you're never going to get inside this cookie jar, I'll stick to Sandoval."

Sandoval revealed a devilish grin. "Never say never, Mari."

7

A MAN WHO KNOWS WHAT HE WANTS

*T*wo months later

    "Come on," she urged as she begged for the sky to stay dark.

She'd been undercover for two months now but had no significant intel to report.

To make matters worse, Bear's surveillance of her had only increased since their altercation.

She'd become accustomed to moving around the guards since she'd secured a short band radio and picked up their frequency, tracking their comings and goings.

Being in the field meant long periods of radio silence, she understood that. It took time to create a meaningful relationship with the target. But her instincts told her that she was being left in the dark. Not just by the Syndicate, but the agency as well. *Bear might be undercover too! where you really is!*

She decided to reach out to her base and give them an update. She'd used her newly-acquired radio to escape the villa undetected and had reached the Agency's safe house, where she could make the call using the burner phone stashed there.

"Omicron, this is Zero."

"One moment, Zero." There was a brief pause while she was being connected. "Zero, this is Caldwell. What in the hell is going on?"

"It's hard to explain, sir."

"Then use small words."

"I don't have time to tell you everything that's going on. The major issue is Sandoval. He wants to trust me, but he's still being cautious. The pop quizzes from his lackeys about the technology have slowed down, so Xavion's boot camp worked wonders."

"Good, now what can you tell us about his operation?"

"Not much more than you already know. It's serious, and everyone is tight-lipped about it. Right now, all I know is that the Algorithm has several components to it. He has some important people regularly coming on to his yacht. He's in good with the prime minister."

"That makes sense. We've tried through official diplomatic channels to enter Turks and Caicos but have been rejected each time."

"That tracks. He has a weekly one-on-one meeting with the prime minister. After those, he meets with his inner circle. The only person in the circle I can confirm is Bear, his enforcer. I can only get away every now and then, thanks to the cleaning and grounds staff, but I gotta be careful how I move. I can't stay here for long."

"Zero, this is Xavion. Sandoval has an EMP minefield with a five-mile radius set up on the yacht. Every time we get near it, all our devices stop. We can't get close to it. We've talked to the prime minister, but as you pointed out, he's clearly in Sandoval's back pocket. We need you to figure out what's on that yacht."

"I'm on it, but it's not gonna be easy. I've only seen Sandoval and Bear go on it. Hell, I still haven't found Hummingbird."

"We have to assume she's dead now," Caldwell interjected.

"I've built a relationship with the housekeeping team, so I can move in and out of the villa with a little more help, but it's infrequent at best, and not for long periods of time. Usually the opportunity only comes when Bear and Sandoval are on the mega yacht."

"So, they're on the yacht right now?" Caldwell asked.

"They should be back shortly. In fact, I can't stay much longer," she replied.

Xavion chimed in. "Zero, can you confirm they're working on the Algorithm in the villa at all? Our drones can't get through the EMPs."

"From what I can tell, nothing is happening at the villa. Hell, I can't even confirm this man is a terrorist. So far, I haven't seen him do anything out of the ordinary. He's rational, levelheaded and... kind."

"He may be those things, but don't lose sight of the fact that he's our target," Caldwell said.

"Roger that."

"Stay the course, Zero. Do whatever you need to gain access to the yacht. If you can do that, then maybe we'll figure something out."

Shanice hung up the phone. She had to get back to the villa now.

She scurried over to the moped she'd secured and darted back to the villa. As she snuck through the staff entrance and back into her room, she thought back on the last two months.

Everything had been quiet. Sandoval seemed to have more interest in getting in her pants than he did taking over the world. In fact, there was nothing to show he'd been planning *anything* outside of her abduction. Yet the very fact they abducted her meant there was more going on. *Sounds like another test – will she sleep w/ him to get intel*

She had to be patient. For the past two months, she'd been spending time with Sandoval and getting to know him. He'd been extremely transparent, and yet closed. She genuinely liked him. In another life, she could have been his friend. Still, her mission was to figure out his plan.

The sun was beginning to rise as she got dressed. She went to their daily breakfast spot, where he'd often surprise her with flowers or perfume or exquisite food he'd cooked himself. Each day she'd be curious what he would have in store.

She walked into the main room, but Sandoval was nowhere to be found.

He should've been back from the yacht by now. This would be an excellent opportunity to see where he slept.

She walked toward his quarters in the compound. The room she knew to be his had double doors with heavy black door knockers. One door was partially opened, so she peeked in to see if she could find anything. At the room's entrance sat a table, a small box with her alias on it.

For Mari.

He's persistent, if nothing else.

She picked up the box and opened it. There was a bottle of perfume inside.

"It's Versace Light Blue. It's not a very expensive scent, but I love it. I think it would smell wonderful on you."

The voice behind her came from nowhere, but she worked hard to internalize her shock, instead acting as if she were meant to be in the room. "I'm not wearing anything you gave one of your groupies, am I?"

"What? No. Chill out, man," he joked.

Shanice sprayed the scent and inhaled.

She looked forward to his daily experiments in courtship.

I have to play the role. No one said I couldn't enjoy it.

"Well?" he prompted.

She looked coyly at him and didn't respond. Instead, she looked at the bottle. It smelled just as good as the other four he'd bought her – which was four more than any other man had. *R these scents is nother liked?*

She inhaled again and fell in love with its light floral scent.

Shanice glanced at Sandoval, who was smiling knowingly. He knew she loved it, but she wouldn't give him the satisfaction of admitting it.

She simply shrugged. "It's alright."

His advances were romantic and thoughtful.

She'd been in foxholes with twenty men, associated with military generals from foreign countries, and won every battle she'd ever been a part of, except for the battle with her inner schoolgirl – what she called the hopeless romantic inside of her. The version of her that used to listen to Boyz II Men's song, On Bended Knee, and dream that Marcus Winters would feel that way about her.

Sandoval wasn't running the game. He truly liked her, and she knew it. Still, she couldn't fall for him; he was the mission.

Sandoval walked over and whispered in her ear, "It's cute that you think you can friendzone me forever. I like a challenge, and nothing in life worth having comes easy."

"So, I'm a challenge?"

"You are, but I've always known it's hard to hunt a lioness," he said, bowing sarcastically.

Shanice smirked. "Oh, so I guess that makes you a lion?"

Sandoval righted himself and leaned closer to her. "Not just a lion. It makes me *your* lion, Mari."

She stepped away from him.

Focus on the mission.

He wore his confidence like cologne, and it smelled incredible. Her eyes softened as Sandoval continued. "I don't know if you've ever had a man be this certain that he wants to be with you, but I promise you, he'll never fight harder than me to prove it."

His certainty and persistence flattered her.

Sandoval stepped away as she asked, "Well, Mister Lion, how do I know you're not just sniffing around for some of this kitty cat?"

"For you to even ask me that tells me you don't understand how I feel."

"And how do you feel?"

"Like a man looking at a woman he wants to love." *Oop!*

His words caught her off guard.

He'd never disguised his intent with her. She decided she could use this to her advantage to gain access to the yacht. But it was a dangerous game.

She looked at him and, for the first time, gave him something he'd been longing for: honesty. "Sando— Adonis... you're nothing like I imagined."

"What did you imagine?"

"A cold, calculated man. Never this genuine or sensitive."

Sandoval put his hand on her cheek, drawing her closer with the other. "I've been told I can be those things, but in my heart I'm very passionate about challenges and the things I care about. You fall into both categories."

"But why me?"

41

"Why not you? You don't think I see you? You wear a mask, Mari, to hide who you are. But I see you."

His words were dangerously alluring.

"It's been three months, and I haven't stopped showering you with affection. The only person who doesn't see that is you. The question is, why do you think it should be someone else? Why isn't this the moment that you find love? Mari, make no mistake, I've been waiting for you since the moment I saw you in the coffee shop."

Shanice welled up at the sincerity in his words. His plans were such a deep secret, but his heart was an open book. She knew she wasn't really the Mari he loved, but it felt wonderful to be appreciated, valued, catered to, and respected.

Focus on the mission.

She wanted to walk away, but her legs wouldn't carry her. She wanted to push away, but her arms wouldn't let go of him.

She wanted to kiss him, so she did.

He returned her passion with all the pent up desire he'd been building up over the past three months.

Suddenly he pulled away, holding her at arm's length. "Mari... are you sure this is what you want?"

She pulled him in and kissed him again.

It didn't matter what she wanted. She yearned to finally know what it felt like to be touched by a man who looked at her the way he did.

The two kissed passionately. Shanice pushed him down onto the bed and slid his pants off. She climbed on top of him, grinding her most sensitive parts against his hard wood. The two kissed with the fury of two lovers held apart for too long.

Sandoval flipped her over to her back and lowered his head to her pussy. She moaned in ecstasy as she grabbed at his locked hair. She felt his warm lips wrap tightly around her clit, which was swelling with pleasure.

"Oh, shit!" she moaned as she dug her nails into his back.

He persisted, licking her wet pussy until she could no longer stand the pleasure.

She gasped for air as she came, but still he persisted in licking her. The sensation was almost unbearable, yet she was climaxing again.

She thought she couldn't take any more, but Sandoval had a way with his tongue, allowing her just enough time to catch her breath before going again. By the third one, she was quivering and sensitive to the touch.

Sandoval moved up her body before flipping them again, thrusting inside her. As she rode his rock hard dick, he moaned savagely as he erupted inside of her. Hope they put you on bc

Fully satisfied, the two of them held each other until slumber came.

8

WATER WORLD

"That's nice," Shanice moaned as she closed her eyes and let the water from the shower stream keep her warm. She had already washed up, and just wanted a quiet place to get her thoughts in order. The only place she'd ever been able to do that was in the water; it provided clarity.

She smiled as vivid memories of her childhood filled her mind. She remembered being on a boat with her mother when she was eight, and how the mist of the saltwater felt against her face.

She recalled the day her father taught her how to swim. His smile when she finally figured it out. She missed them both intensely.

She remembered taking up swimming when she got to the States, because being underwater was the only place she could scream with nobody noticing. She became so good at it, she eventually broke her high school's all-time 100m record.

Beautiful!
Ooh...
oicnorian

All of that led to her joining the Army. She was probably better suited for the Navy, but she'd known that if she wanted to join the CIA, she'd have to see action. Every decision she'd made had brought her to this point, and none of this was like she'd imagined.

I slept with the target. Who does that? *a good operative*
She shook her head and thought about the morning.

It had been six months since she'd slept with anyone, and the person she breaks the drought with is the person she was literally spying on. *[handwritten: !OMG WTF Norah? Lol]*

She looked at her crotch and slapped it like a toddler who had just got in trouble. "What's wrong with you?" she scolded.

She didn't regret the act itself, more her lack of professionalism. She was on assignment, and the sheer nature of her duties were designed for her to keep her guard up, but she'd slipped.

Thing is, I don't even know why.

Sure, Sandoval was attractive, but she was already compartmentalizing her feelings for Marcus. They both had similar personalities. Sandoval reminded her of Marcus' fighting spirit and dogged persistence.

He'll figure it out. He's got to.

"You okay, love?"

She looked over as Sandoval opened the door and walked in. His chiseled, naked body looked like it had been constructed by the Greek gods.

As he stepped into the shower, she put her hands on his bare chest. "I was just thinking about your sexy British accent, and your perfectly chiseled chest, that's all."

"Well, I can stop working out and get flubby if you want."

"What did you just say?"

"I can get flubby."

"You mean 'flabby.'" *[handwritten: I would have said fluffy, Lol]*

"You Americans with your backwards talk." *[handwritten: Lol]*

The two laughed as they embraced and kissed passionately. Sandoval picked up the soap and washed his muscular frame. Shanice took the wash cloth from him and took over. As he stood in the shower and closed his eyes, she tracked *[handwritten: traced?]* each cut in his physique.

For now, she was just going to live in the moment.

"And for the record, I don't have an accent," he said, cutting off her train of thought.

"Oh, you definitely have an accent. It's obvious when you say certain words, like 'mum.'"

"What's wrong with that? How are you supposed to say it."

"Mom, or momma."

"You're from the Caribbean though, right? I would think 'mommy' would be your word of choice."

"How do you know I'm from—"

"It's in your features. You have the same cheekbones me mu... I mean, my momma had."

She laughed as he kissed her neck and said, "I wanted to thank you for this morning. You were incredible, and I hope—"

"There it goes. Did you see that?"

"See what?"

"See what I mean when I say that you're out here trying too hard?"

"I don't under—"

"Why are you thanking me for sex? I liked it, so did you. Why don't you just act like every other man in recorded history and be an asshole?"

Sandoval stepped back to his side of the shower. "Because I'm not like every other man, Mari. In fact, let's be clear about something. I don't appreciate the projection."

"Excuse me?"

"We've been together every day for the past three months. I've shown interest and you've acknowledged it, but like a cat. I never know when you're going to strike."

Shanice splashed water at him playfully, and he moved back under the shower spray with her. "I'm not that bad."

"You are, but it's fine, I can take it. Look, I can't control how other men have talked to you in the past, but this is how I'm going to talk to you. It costs me nothing to pay you a compliment, and we can all afford to hear nice things about ourselves, so why can't we use this as the currency it was intended to be?"

She was silent, pondering his words.

"What I'm saying is, if you think this is me trying too hard, maybe it's really that your past lovers haven't tried hard enough."

She processed his words. She'd let her guard down once, but she wouldn't let it happen again.

Playing the role, she wrapped her hands around his neck and looked into his eyes. "So, we're lovers now?"

"We did just make love."

"What if this was just a sport fuck?"

"You're not the kind of woman who sport fucks."

"How do you kno— "

"Because if you were, we'd still be sport fucking, instead of having this conversation. You're a woman coming to grips with the fact you've spent a lifetime dealing with substandard men, so all this black excellence is a little intimidating. But don't worry, I don't bite – unless you want me to."

"Kiss my ass, Sandoval," she said playfully.

In seconds, he spun her around and went to his knees. He pressed his lips against her left cheek, kissing her gently, and did the same to her right.

She looked over her shoulders to watch him right as he looked up at her, smiling devilishly. He spread her cheeks and licked her feverishly.

"Oh, damn," she moaned. "You eating it like groceries, Sandy." She moaned louder as he pressed his tongue into her.

Sandoval nudged her to lean against the wall as he moved his tongue from her ass to her soaking-wet pussy. He slapped her ass as he buried his tongue inside of her.

He abruptly stood up, allowing her to catch her breath. "I just wanted to taste you. When you tell me to kiss your ass, I most certainly will."

"Point taken."

"Today I want to show you something. Get dressed and we'll take a stroll."

She exited the shower and grabbed a towel, heading to pick out her outfit for the day.

She was about to strip off her towel when she saw Bear sitting in the corner of the room.

"Bear! What in the hell?"

Bear stood up and walked over to her. "You won't be wearing that. Sandoval needs to speak to everyone, and he wants you by his side."

Bear put down a box.

Shanice opened it to find a black dress with long sleeves, and a mask similar to the one he wore on the video sent to the Agency.

She lifted the mask to her face.

Bear moved next to her. "You know he'll never love you, right? You're just a tool to help him cope with his misplaced grief."

Before she could respond, he walked out of the room.

Dead mother?

9

WE ARE SEVEN

"*H*ow do I look?" she asked as she twirled in the exquisite black dress.

Sandoval walked over and kissed her on the shoulder. "You look like the queen you are."

As he finished getting ready in his all black tux, she decided this was the perfect opportunity to get an otherwise-guarded man to divulge a bit more on the organization.

"So, why did you choose the name the Seven Syndicate in the first place?" she asked. *deadly welfer to lie*

Sandoval paused for a beat, then resumed getting dressed. "There were originally seven of us: myself and six other men. One of those men was a Colombian freedom fighter named Sandoval."

"Wait, I thought Sandoval was just your online name?"

"It is, but it's also my title. When we formed the Seven Syndicate, we were all idealists. We wanted to change the world. We would blackmail billionaires for money or political leverage, but the thing we learned quickly was, when you're going up against bad people, sometimes you have to be even worse. It wasn't long before we needed trained mercenaries to protect us.

"Sandoval eventually realized we could go after our enemies

before they even thought to come for us. Together, we built an army of mercenaries to help us stabilize countries that the superpowers were trying to destabilize."

He put on his cuff links as he continued. "There are two things they never tell you about power, the first of which is how addictive it becomes. Sandoval's ego grew, and slowly he started abusing the power we'd worked so hard to gain. Our actions were no longer justified by our means. We were just criminals.

"One day, the council decided we needed new leadership. They voted for me. I rejected it immediately; I didn't want to face the wrath of Sandoval. Come to find out, somebody leaked the meeting details to Sandoval, and he walked through the door.

"So, the seven of us were there, half standing with Sandoval, the other half against. And I had the same feelings I had when I saw Tariq X bullying Bear."

Sandoval poured himself a glass of whiskey and took a sip. "I killed him. It was the only way it could end. They installed me as the new leader of the syndicate."

"What happened to the other members?"

"The moment I became Sandoval, I knew the others saw it as a power grab, and it was only a matter of time before those same men were in a dimly-lit room talking about me. I started making plans to eliminate them all. It took some time, but eventually, the only voice anyone would listen to, or even remember, was mine. I was *the* Sandoval."

"It just seems a little hypocritical; you preach about how you hate the abuse of power, yet you seized this organization by force."

"That's the second thing they don't teach you about power: once you have it, you have to do ugly things to keep it. I never wanted to stay Sandoval. I wanted to build a network that would eliminate the need for a Sandoval."

"What makes you think the world needs you?" she asked inquisitively.

He smirked, but didn't respond.

Bear walked up to the pair, interrupting their conversation. "Sandoval, it's time."

The two touched heads and embraced. Sandoval then turned to kiss Shanice before addressing Bear. "Take care of her."

Bear nodded.

Taking Sandoval's lead, everyone put on their masks.

Wearing the same mask as the staff allowed him to blend into the hacker community. He made it a point to hide in plain sight by pretending to be one of the groundskeepers. In truth, no one knew who Sandoval was except a handful of his most trusted men. *But your suite!?*

She admired his cleverness. When she'd met him, he'd looked like he was getting coffee for Bear. Many assumed incorrectly when they saw him carry bags or helping servers; they only saw him as the help.

He enjoyed being invisible; it was one of his strengths. Another was speaking.

He used a voice modulator to hide any remnants of his accent as the video feed started and his image was transmitted around the world. His closest allies were gathered in the room.

"Someone recently asked me, what makes me think the world needs me? And it made me think. What gives me the audacity to think the world needs me? I'm just an average person. But my response is this: tell that to the ten million online. If God didn't favor common people, he wouldn't have made so many of us."

The crowd roared in approval.

Shanice looked at a nearby monitor to confirm Sandoval's number of ten million. The number was now twelve million and counting, all untraceable on the dark web. *What is the dark web? Has a separate http:// address? Seems like reg-web is corrupt enough*

"For far too long, the world leaders have watched those with nothing fight for their very existence on Earth, while they live in luxury. These motherfuckers are even trying to charge you for the bloody sun now. We pay for water as if somebody owns it. They pollute our air without our consent, and we're stuck with the consequences. I say 'we' because I once had nothing. People who have never stepped foot outside their shiny castles made my climb incredibly hard."

The crowd cheered in response to his words. He raised his hand to calm them before continuing. "What they don't know is, we don't want to take the castle. We want to burn the goddamn place to the ground."

The crowd erupted.

She'd only seen this type of reaction to celebrity pastors. His charisma was undeniable.

"The hour of reckoning for those in power is here. They can feel their strength fleeing. They look for us, claiming that we're hiding. I say, they haven't looked hard enough, because we're everywhere. The Algorithm is almost complete, and soon we will show the world the face of the Seven Syndicate.

"So, when I think about the question, what makes me think the world needs me, my answer is simple: it doesn't. But it does need each one of you, and I promise you this: when the day of reckoning comes, no one will ever again ask those kinds of questions to average people."

The crowd chanted his name as he raised both hands in the air in thanks.

He walked off the stage and over to Shanice. "That's what makes me think the world needs me."

She nodded. It had been three months, but this was her first time seeing the true power of the organization and, judging by the size of the crowd, the CIA had severely underestimated Sandoval's reach.

1 0

HUMMINGBIRD

*S*ix weeks later.

Shanice basked in the feel of the saltwater on her skin as she headed back to shore.

She stepped out of the ocean to meet Sandoval, who was standing ready to give her a towel.

They were on the most secluded part of the island. Over the past six weeks, she'd tried to gain access to the yacht, but her efforts just ended up with her making love to Sandoval almost every night.

She took the towel as she examined his strong stature, and the very thought of this dreadlocked man filling her with his manhood was making her wet. *might want to address bc. Y'all never mention*

Think of something else. *it in romance stories or periods*

She tried, but her mind could only think of the darker side of their whirlwind romance.

Can't think about that. Focus on the mission.

The words had become her mantra.

She had worked with the CIA before and understood all their protocols, but she hadn't expected to have feelings for the target.

In truth, she'd been too tired to focus on the mission lately. *prego?*

She spent her nights listening to 90s R&B, soaking in the feeling of the endless orgasms. It was pointless trying to trace his movements. Anytime he went to the yacht, he was always very well guarded, and they would sail the boat no less than half a mile away every night. The guards on the boat had gold insignias on their mask, which she'd deducted gave them special access. They were faceless and nameless. He even had regular conversations with the prime minister, who protected him. He was as insulated as anyone could be.

She walked up the stairs to the villa's patio. The rustic red cobblestone floor burned her feet as she trotted over to the cabana Sandoval was sitting in. He was looking at a monitor and drinking a glass of whiskey.

This is new.

Sandoval was always careful to guard his work, yet it seemed he'd grown comfortable around her.

She leaned in gingerly to get a closer look. There was a man wearing a mask – his mask.

"Is that a fake Sandoval?" she asked.

Sandoval nodded silently, then looked back at the monitor.

There were two people on the screen. The imposter's posture was easily recognizable as Bear. But the person tied to the chair was a surprise: the prime minister of Turks and Caicos.

Without provocation, the impostor stepped forward and slapped the prime minister.

While she couldn't tell what the impostor was saying, it looked to be a stern warning, and the prime minister looked deathly afraid.

She looked at the real Sandoval, confused. "What am I watching here?"

Sandoval leaned over and kissed her. "Well, today the prime minister delivered some very unfortunate news, and I wanted to slap the shit out of him. But then I realized how much time and energy it would take for me to actually go and slap him, when instead I could be on the patio watching you swim. So, I had my body double do it for me."

you are not Bear

"Okay, there's so much to unpack there that I'm sure you won't be forthcoming about, so let me just start with the least-odd thing in that statement. You have a body double?"

He chuckled and winked at her. "I have two body doubles. They've studied my mannerisms. It gives me the ability to blend in."

"Or be in two or three places at once."

"Brilliant, and correct. It's how I get to move among the coders and help staff here, because sometimes when you're the man on top, the only way you can hear the people below you is to walk among them." True!

He had a powerful silence that she admired. He enjoyed being behind the scenes. Never drawing too much attention to himself. It was how he'd avoided the CIA for years.

She thought about the day they'd first met, and how she'd assumed he worked for Bear. He had appeared non-threatening, as beautiful as nightshade.

She looked at the monitor, paying close attention to the mask, and noticed something was different.

"Do they have a duplicate mask?"

"Why did you ask that?"

"From what I could tell, yours is the only one that has the silver rimming around it."

The words caught him off guard, and he looked surprised.

Shanice realized her military attention to detail may have been exposed, and blurted out, "What? I pay attention to my man."

Sandoval's suspicion turned to excitement. "I'm your man now?"

"As much as you're sticking your dick inside me, you better be." !

Sandoval grinned from ear to ear, standing up and pumping his fist in the air.

Shanice couldn't help but be flattered at his childlike joy. She pressed on. "Quit being silly and answer my question, Sandy."

"Well, my lady, they have slight duplicates. When they wear the mask, the modulator activates."

"How did you come up with the idea to add silver trim to your mask, and why silver instead of gold?"

ooh! Norian Preach!

"It's a message, to the faithful and the fruitful. Too many people miss the silver lining because they're expecting gold."

It was exactly what she'd come to expect from Sandoval. He was profoundly subtle.

While it impressed her, she also realized this was the first time he'd been this open since they'd met.

This is useful intel.

She pressed for more. "What if one of your doubles steals your actual mask?"

"Oh, I run all these masks on biometrics. My skin, sweat, and breath are kind of like an 'on' switch. If someone puts on an inactivated mask, it releases a poison. Once that happens, the mask sends an alert to me."

"That sounds like overkill."

"You say that, but these precautions are necessary. We've had people try to infiltrate us. We're not easily fooled. As a matter of fact, we had a woman – a brilliant coder – who tried to steal a mask and enter a restricted area of the villa. The moment she took a breath, the mask locked around her neck. The masks have a failsafe – HQ intercepted the communication system in her stolen mask, asking her personal security questions she couldn't answer. When she failed the security parameters, the mask shut down any intake of oxygen.

"She suffocated."

Well, the disappearance of Hummingbird was solved.

He wanted her to know; he was opening up because he trusted her, and she felt terrible because she needed to report all of this to her team.

The man next to her was as strategic as they come. It was no wonder he was steps ahead of every government agency. He thought about things in a way that no one could imagine.

"That is some next level shit. Where did you get these?"

Without looking up Sandoval smirked. "I invented it."

She'd known he was smart, but not this level. He was a genius. A self-made man.

Still flustered by his announcement, she blurted out in a faux English accent, "Are you bloody serious, Governor?"

Sandoval laughed and took a shot of whiskey. "Mari, I'm sure you're an amazing coder, but respectfully, your skill isn't anywhere near my level." ~ So why outsource? Why not do it yourself with

The pair laughed as she pinched his shoulder. all the fail safes you can

"It's why I stopped questioning the hackers a long time ago. think of? Anything you could possibly come up with would sound childish compared to what I've done. And to be clear, I didn't want you to feel it was because you're a woman, because it's not. I'm just so much further ahead than anyone you will ever meet when it comes to technology, that it's embarrassing – and I say that with all modesty."

"I can feel the modesty in the room with us."

"I know you're saying that sarcastically, but trust me, I was being modest."

"Really?"

"Yes, love, I cannot overstate how good I am."

She smirked at his confidence, but she believed him. It saddened her that, with all his abilities, he'd chosen this route. Looking at him endearingly, she stroked his hair. "How did you end up like this?"

"Like what?"

"Wounded. You could've done anything in the world, *been* anything in the world. Why did you choose… this?"

He contemplated her question. She could see the wheels turning in his head as he searched for the answer. After a moment, he said, "We all have things that shape us, you know? Like, a kid could be a Harvard graduate or a hardened criminal. It's all based on their choices, and those choices are primarily based on the things that took root from their environment."

"So, for you, it was your environment?"

"Definitely. Growing up, it was just my mum and me. She was a wonderful lady, but we were extremely poor. My dad would come around every week or so, but he never had much interest in me. He'd take his rum, go in the back room with me mum. When he was finished, he'd come out to ask me how school was.

"That was the extent of our relationship. When you're eight, you think that's just the way dads are. Thing is, I was so excited for him to ask me about school. I'd wait all week for him to ask me that question. I worked really hard so that, when he asked me, I'd always have something amazing to tell him. He'd smile and say, 'The kid's smart', or pat me on the head, and it meant the world to me."

He took another sip of the whiskey and let out a deep sigh. "Until I was about twelve, when mum got sick. She told me I was going to live with my dad. I realized then how little I knew about him. I was devastated because I didn't want to lose my mother, but as her death became inevitable, I looked for the silver lining, which was getting to know my dad."

Sandoval took a sip of this whiskey as a tear rolled from his eye. She'd tugged on a very painful thread.

She rubbed his back as he continued.

"When my mother passed away, I left the funeral with my dad. That was the silver lining. We got in his car and drove to a KFC – for some reason that place was wildly popular in the U.K. Then we ordered the food, sat down, and I thought to myself, *finally we'll have more to talk about than school*, you know? He'll tell me something I didn't know about my mom, or the rules in his house, didn't matter what; for the first time in my life, my conversation with him would be something different.

"So, we get to the KFC. When I sit down, he tells me to go wash my hands, he'll be back – he'd left something outside. Only he never came back. I looked outside in the parking lot and his car was gone. The hardest day of my life, and he just left me there. I figured it out when I noticed the KFC was a block away from a homeless shelter."

He wiped a tear from his eye as he spoke. More tears followed as he continued.

"To make matters worse, when I got to the shelter, there were no beds. Luckily, the on-duty staff could tell I was at rock bottom, and was kind enough to let me sleep on the floor in the office area."

"Your father is a horrible person," Shanice said.

He chuckled. "As fate would have it, I was right in the middle of my silver lining. The night I stayed there, the printer stopped working, and no one knew how to get it back online. I'm not sure how, but I fixed the problem, and I fell in love with computers. That skill, more than anything, has kept me alive. It changed everything for me."

"And that's how you got here."

"Believe me, I didn't think it would all turn out this way. You know, we were so poor in a land with so much. We'd get on the bus, or walk, and everyone had nice cars, and I didn't understand why that wasn't my life. I didn't understand why my father left me that day – though I later learned it was because my mother was his mistress, and he didn't want to explain my existence to his wife." *Oh hence weekly visits*

"Again, horrible person."

"You'll get no argument from me there. But, when you're poor, all you can see are the things you don't have that everyone else does. I think the day I met Bear was the first time everything came together. I realized that if you don't fight back, you're dead.

"When I think about the way things are in the world, it's no different from the con man taking everything away from Bear. Thinking back on it, I've always been the kid to bring a brick to the party to smash guys like that in the face. Only this time I'm throwing a brick at the world."

She understood him a little too well.

She saw now his every step to running a criminal empire, and she wasn't entirely sure he was wrong. In the Army, it was easy to shoot first and ask questions later. But being in the CIA was deeper. You had to gain trust, be vulnerable – and right now she was very vulnerable.

Sandoval wiped his face from any remaining tears. "What about you?"

"What about me?"

"Oh, you don't get me to open up about the heavy stuff and just walk away, love. Why are you the way you are?"

She knew what he was asking. He needed honesty.

"You mean why am I angry? Well, I know it has to do with my parents. When I first lost them, I went through all the stages of grief; I tried to rationalize it, I wanted to end it all, I wondered *why my parents?* Maybe I needed to find the terrorist who did this and hold them accountable.

"But the more time passed, the more I realized I was wrong. This goddamn lottery of rich and poor, that's what killed my parents, and that's what I want to burn down."

Shanice watched as Sandoval nodded his head in understanding.

"And since they've been gone, sometimes I feel like... maybe the real me isn't good enough. I'm afraid the real me is unlovable. Maybe that's why my parents died, you know? I think sometimes I've been medicating that hurt with aggression since the day they died. Because I'm angry."

Sandoval leaned across the table and held her chin with his fingers. "Listen to me, Mari. You can't ever be unlovable, because I'm here and I'm always gonna love you."

The pair exchanged a kiss.

In another life, those words would have been reassuring, but they were built on the foundation of a lie. She knew there was no world in which the words could be true.

She wiped her own tears.

"I need to leave."

11
SWEETEST TABOO

"*L*eave? I don't understand."

"Don't take this the wrong way, but I just…"

"What?"

"When things get heavy like this, I need to get some air. You know what I mean? I need to walk and talk and be alone. I can't do that here. I just want to grab a cup of coffee in a café and read a good book, or walk the promenade. I just miss them both so much."

Sandoval kissed her. "You know leaving the compound is against the rules, but since I make the rules, I say we get ready to go into town."

She nodded as he wrapped his bulging arms around her and kissed her on the side of her neck.

"Besides, today is our last day in Turks, so let's make the most of it."

His words snapped her back to reality.

She needed to find a way to let Omicron know what was happening.

The pair, along with Bear, took a car into town. During the drive, she thought about how she could slip away.

She'd compartmentalized her feelings during this assignment, but her walls were crumbling. The deeper she became involved with Sandoval, the more she was losing herself. Honestly, she sympathized with his position. From his point of view, he wasn't the bad guy. He was the guy with the brick in his hand trying to save the less fortunate.

As they pulled up, she saw her opportunity to leave.

She squeezed his thigh. "Love, pull over here. Since we're leaving, I want to get a few souvenirs. I've always wanted to stop by this shop. I'll meet you at the coffee house if that's okay with you."

"Absolutely, love. I can have Bear escort—"

"I don't need Bear standing over me while I look for gifts. I won't be long. I just need to— "

He grasped her hand. "I understand." She knew Sandoval had no interest in shopping; it was the perfect cover.

"Thank you."

"No offense, but shopping really isn't my thing."

She kissed him on the cheek as the car stopped a block from the coffee shop. She exited the car with a wave to Sandoval and walked into the store, appearing to look for souvenirs.

She needed to contact base to let them know what was about to happen

She picked up a seashell and was about to ask the shop owner for his phone when she heard a familiar voice.

"That's a mighty fine seashell for your boyfriend."

Shanice spun around to face the familiar voice, stunned. "Hal w— what are you doing here?"

"I'm doing the same thing you're doing here. Or at least I hope I am."

"Your teacher says you haven't called home in over three weeks."

"You know it's hard for me to check in. I'm always studying."

"That's what we assumed, but the professor wants me to make sure you're still attending our college."

Shanice glared at him.

She pulled him to a secluded corner. "Are you questioning my loyalty?"

"Wouldn't have to if you turned in a report every now and then."

She closed her eyes and shook her head. "For starters, Hummingbird is dead. She suffocated after stealing one of their biometric masks."

"Okay, that's a start. She wasn't one of ours, but it's still evidence. Do you know what they did with the body?"

"No. Listen, Sandoval is gonna be here any second. If he catches you, both our bodies will end up with Hummingbird's."

Hal stood still. "You never answered my question."

"Fine, if you need to say it, I'll say it." She reached out and shook Hal's hand. "I'm with you all the way. You happy now?"

"I think you needed to hear yourself say it."

The pair walked out of the store to the corner of the street so Shanice could keep an eye out for Sandoval or his driver. "What's that supposed to mean?"

"I've seen the two of you holding hands, and I've seen the way you look at him."

His statement shocked her. "You've been spying on me?"

"Yes, Zero, I'm a spy. So are you. That's what we do at the Agency. We observe and report, of which you've done neither."

"It's not easy to—"

"You wouldn't be here if the job were easy, so save the horseshit. I'm here because you two look like a couple of lovebirds on a honeymoon."

The words stung. She fired back. "Look, I didn't ask for this assignment. You could've just as easily stuck me in a hole in Siberia instead of a tropical island. And I'm not an idiot, either."

"What's that supposed to mean?"

"It means you want me to believe it's dumb luck that I just so happen to look like the target's long-deceased mother?"

"What? We knew nothing about Sandoval."

"Now who's spouting horseshit?"

"Look, whether we did or not is irrelevant now. We need to know why the prime minister stopped by the compound this morning."

63

"Here's what I know: we're leaving today. Apparently, he had a run in with the prime minister and he's packing up camp."

"How are you leaving?"

"I'm assuming by water. He told his enforcer to tell everyone we're getting on a yacht and leaving. He didn't say where, but judging by the look on your face, you already know."

Hal looked around to make sure there were no wandering eyes and stepped closer to Shanice. "There are six other yachts identical to the one at the villa, all anchored around the island."

"Hold on, there are seven yachts? They've gotta be decoys. How did you guys miss that?"

"We screwed the pooch on that one. We had the island under routine surveillance, but by the time we made the connection, all six yachts had arrived."

Shanice rolled her eyes and shook her head. "You've got to be kidding me. You're worried about me doing my job, yet you let six identical yachts come to an island that happens to harbor a terrorist you're pursuing?"

"Like you said, the man is smart. Four of the yachts showed up over the last year at different times, before we had a clue where he was. One came before you got the assignment. And the last two showed up sparingly. By the time we noticed the pattern, it was too late."

"Yeah, keep telling yourself that. This assignment was built on a hope and a prayer, and you know it. Hell, I've been there for five months, and the worst thing I've seen is him sending a body double to slap a man."

"Look, we can sort this out later. This guy might be innocent, he might not be, but the question you have to ask yourself is: if it comes down to it, will you be able to pull the trigger?"

Shanice didn't have time to respond as she noticed Bear approaching, quickly followed by Sandoval.

She turned back to Hal and exclaimed while pointing, "So just three blocks up, you can't miss it."

"Thanks, ma'am," Hal smiled as he walked off.

Shanice turned around to find Sandoval standing in front of her with her coffee. "Two creams, two sugars."

"Just the way I like it. Thank you."

"Ready to roll?"

"Yeah."

The pair walked towards the car and sipped their coffees when Sandoval asked, "Who was that gentleman you were talking to?"

"Just a tourist looking for directions back to his hotel."

Sandoval pondered that. "Did you give him what he needed?"

"I hope so. You know I don't know how to get anywhere in this town, I haven't spent much time in it. Where are we headed to next?"

"There's been a change of plans, love. We have to head back to the villa now."

The trip back to the villa was quiet.

She thought about her time as Mari Patterson, the hacker who spent her days on a tropical island. Hal's words rang in her head. Mari was in a relationship, a great one. Spending this time with Sandoval, she found a comfort in him she'd never known.

Still, he was an enigma. He never developed patterns to discover or left any detail unattended. And the habits he had were strict. He was always one step ahead of everyone.

She wondered if his chivalrous act was a ruse.

Why wouldn't he be lying? I am.

But the longer she thought about it, the less black-and-white everything seemed. Despite everything going on, he had won her heart. In any other life, Sandoval would be the perfect gentleman. He was compassionate and thoughtful, but the thorns of living had cut him deeply. There was a deep hurt inside of him, a hurt only he and Bear knew.

Still, she couldn't get Hal's words out of her mind.

If it comes down to it, will you be able to pull the trigger?

12

RULES OF ENGAGEMENT

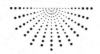

"So, where are we going?" Shanice asked.

It was two hours into the trip. They'd climbed aboard the yacht at the villa and immediately set sail, with no other boat in sight. She didn't know where they were headed, and Sandoval seemed to have no interest in telling her.

"Have some wine, baby."

"No, thank you," she responded.

She thought about Hal's words. It was time for her to do her job.

Sandoval lifted the glass. "Are you sure? It's Black Girl Magic and—"

"Do you trust me?"

"What?" Sandoval was surprised by her words.

"Do you trust me?"

"Of course. I... Where is this coming from?"

"For months I've been by your side, sharing your bed, not asking any questions. You paid me to do a job, and I don't even know what it was. Don't get me wrong, I enjoy your company. I just need to know if this is real to you."

Sandoval put down his glass of whiskey. "Mari, you know you're special to me, right?"

"Am I? Hell, I can't even go outside without supervision."

"That's more for your safety than a lack of—"

"I was taking care of myself long before I met you. I don't need you to do that for me. But that's not the point, Sandy. Seriously, you've spent the last five months on this boat, and I expected to see something – anything – of what you've been doing on this boat, but now I'm starting to wonder if this is where you took another wo—" *play the victim*

good,

"Mari, stop it right now. You know what you're saying is foolishness. Listen, after tomorrow, we can talk about it all. I'm just... being careful."

She stayed silent.

He approached her and slowly wrapped his muscular arms around her. She attempted to resist but it was halfhearted. Eventually, the two settled as he held her, and they watched the sunset.

"You know you mean everything to me, right?" he whispered gently in her ear. His words melted away her defenses.

She sighed. "I know. But your project means everything too. I can't even take a trip to the store without scrutiny."

Sandoval nodded, stroking her arms. "You're right. Allow me to make it up to you."

Sandoval pulled out his phone and put on a playlist. Lucy Pearl's Dance Tonight began playing over the loudspeaker. Shanice loved the song, but she wasn't going to give in to him too easily.

Sandoval danced as if no one was watching. She saw the joy in his eyes and looked at him, rolling her eyes coyly. Still, he continued.

When Just Me and You by Toni Tony Tone came on, she could no longer resist his advances, and joined him as he sang passionately while they danced.

As they moved rhythmically in the sunset, she watched him.

In any other life, this driven man would be king, and she'd be his queen.

"What are you thinking about, beautiful? Are you still mad at me?" he asked as they danced.

She shook her head. "No one has ever treated me this way."

"Well, like I said, I'm a man who knows what he wants. I have no problem spending my time showing you what that means."

"Sandy, I—"

"You don't have to say anything. I heard you earlier. Right now I just want you to dance with me."

Shanice acquiesced.

As they danced, the sun made its departure and gave way to the moon. The irony of Sweetest Taboo by Sade playing wasn't lost on her as he pressed against her body.

She didn't want to resist him. He smelled amazing, and his white linen shirt clung to his ripped chest, showing off his muscles as they moved.

When the song finished, the pair shared a passionate kiss, and she held him as they watched the ocean ripple.

She'd never expected a target of the CIA to be so compassionate and thoughtful. In fact, the only person lying in this relationship was her.

"I know you think you're a prisoner at times, but do you know how I regard the last five months?"

"We went over this when we first met. I can't read minds."

Sandoval chuckled. "Each day I've thought: we're on this beautiful tropical island, and of all God's natural beauties and splendors, the most exotic, breathtaking creature I've seen is standing right in front of me."

Shanice blushed – it was hard not to. She knew he was sincere. Still, she pushed back. "Run that game somewhere else. You just want me to give you pussy, that's all."

"Untrue, though I do love to feel and taste you. But I'm willing to earn that pleasure tonight."

She looked up at him and into his eyes as he brushed a few strands of hair away from her face.

"Then what do you want?" she asked.

He kissed her hands and looked into her eyes. "I want you to give me your heart – all of it – because you already have mine. That's how we gain the trust you're looking for."

She didn't want to resist him. This wasn't the time for espionage, or cloak-and-dagger games. As guilt-ridden as she was, there was no denying she'd become attached to him. He was everything she'd hoped for in a man.

She kissed him on the neck and whispered in his ear. "You're already in my heart. But I don't want to be used and I don't want to be hurt." *oh!*

"It's funny, my mother used to say the same thing to my father."

He released her and glanced at the water, his thoughts as deep as the ocean. She stood next to him in silence.

"You know, you look just like her. Do you think it's weird to love someone that looks like your mother?" *Yes!*

"No, 'cause I'm a bad bitch, and if your momma looked like me then that would make her a bad bitch, and who doesn't want their son to end up with a bad bitch?" *Sure y'all not related? Island hopping*

He laughed at her words then kissed her on her shoulder. "Indeed."

The winds were getting stronger as they sailed, chilling the night. Sandoval moved closer to her to guard her from the wind.

Sandoval was a good man.

Maybe he's being framed.

Everything she'd seen so far was circumstantial. *Girl you don't fall for the. Okey doke. This could be test #2*

She took his glass of whiskey and gulped the remaining liquor, throwing the glass in the ocean. *You got glasses to spare?*

"Sandy, I don't think I've ever felt this way about someone. I haven't felt like this since I was in high school. Thank you for your patience and persistence."

He spun her around into his arms, looking deeply into her eyes. "I love you, Mari. I'm going to give you the entire world."

"Sandy, I...."

She kissed him. Their passion ignited instantly.

He picked her up and carried her to his room, resting her on the bed.

He slowly undressed her, kissing her body as her clothes hit the floor. "Bloody hell, you are so beautiful."

He kissed her neck gently, working his way down to her left

Ooh!, Mr Norian!

breast, his tongue circling her areola, leaving moisture where there was none. He took two fingers and put them in her mouth to moisten, moving them to her throbbing clit, stroking it gently.

She moaned as he kissed his way down her abdomen, and to the outside of her hips, over her thighs. Finally, she moaned in ecstasy as his lips replaced his fingers.

"Damn, Sandy!"

He inhaled deeply as the air cooled her pussy. The heat of his tongue extinguished the coolness as he pressed it against her.

"I could eat you forever," he said, coming up for air.

She looked at her juices saturating his beard and gushed with wetness.

"Give me what I need," she demanded, forcing his head back down.

He obliged. He licked her with passion and intensity as her climax built. It wasn't long before she was moaning, "I'm cumming."

She released her nectar as he continued to indulge in her release.

She eventually pushed his head away. "Damn it, I hate you."

As her body shivered in ecstasy, she rolled to the side to catch her breath.

He pushed her back. "Don't run now, love, we're just getting started."

He buried his mouth on her again. She was almost too sensitive, but his tongue was so soft and gentle, it quickly turned to arousal. He was learning her pussy, responding to her moans, and he was a quick study.

His persistence paid off when she came a second time.

He rubbed his dick as she shivered in pleasure. "I want to feel you."

She nodded. He took off his clothing, exposing his rock-hard dick. His precum dripped from the tip onto the bed.

"Someone's ready," she grinned.

"I can't get enough of you, but you already knew that," he said.

Weird description

He climbed on top of her and slid his heavy dick inside her.

She moaned, still sensitive from her last orgasm, but with each stroke she not only regained desire, but noticed how compassionate he'd been towards her, how protective, how sincere. There was no hint of the monster she was supposed to be hunting.

He slowly pumped his dick inside her wet, warm walls. His pace picked up until he was thrusting up against her g-spot with a reckless force.

She rolled her eyes as she had another orgasm, him not far behind.

"Oh my God, I'm cumming!" he moaned as he released his seed into her pussy.

He collapsed in pleasure, the both of them looking out of the window to the night's sky.

"That was amazing."

"You're amazing, Mari. Were you satisfied?"

"Immensely."

"I need to say something. I believe in God. This wonderful universe, with all of its miracles, did not happen by mistake. I feel like everything we've ever done – or will do – serves God, and I believe the work I have to do benefits all humanity. They say the right people show up in your life at the right time.

"Since the day we met, I've felt like the weight of the world has been lifted from my shoulders. I feel like the universe gifted you to me because you make every moment better. What I'm saying is, I love you, and I don't want you to say it back. Because I don't need you to love me at this moment. I hope and I pray that it happens, but right now, I'm satisfied feeling this way about you."

His words broke her heart. She knew he was telling the truth. What was worse, he'd been a wonderful boyfriend – the best she'd ever had.

But her job was to take him down.

Focus on the mission.

He got pussy whipped. Ready to marry Yu

71

13

RAVEN CLAW

ermuda
"Sandy? Are you awake?"

She looked over at her lover, who was fast asleep in the bed. She glanced out the window, looking for any hint on where they were.

Another island, it looks like. Where in the hell are we?

"Sandy."

She shook him again, a futile attempt. He was in a deep sleep.

She quickly dressed and left their room. When she got to the deck, she looked around. The yacht had docked on a secluded beach.

I need to tell Omicron where we are.

She scanned for the skeleton crew that had sailed them to shore. Most of them were preoccupied with their duties.

Now's my chance.

Shanice crept towards the ramp leading to the dock when she suddenly felt a powerful grip on her arm.

"Just where in the hell do you think you're going?" Bear said, gripping tightly.

She tried to pull away, but it was no use. "Bear, what are you doing?"

"No, the better question is, what are you doing? You know the rules."

"Let her go."

Sandoval approached the two of them.

"Bear, I said, let her go. Mari has proven herself to be one of us."

"Maybe to you, but not to me."

"How is that any of my concern?"

Bear's eyes widened.

He turned to Sandoval and pleaded. "We know nothing about her, Adonis! Listen, mate, you're not thinking clearly. This woman could be anyone, and you're just gonna let her into our—"

"Our what, Bear? What exactly do *we* have? Don't mistake my allowing you to speak your mind as some kind of partnership. You're not the brains of this operation – I am. You do what I say, or you do nothing at all, and right now I'm telling you to let her go."

Bear stared Sandoval down, gnawing at his lip. She brushed up against his side as he released her arm and addressed his friend, "You may be the brains of this operation, but I'm the only one thinking clearly."

He glared at Shanice before he walked off.

Sandoval walked toward her and wrapped an arm around her waist. "Please ignore Bear. We've been through a lot together. He means well, but in our line of business it's hard to trust anyone. He takes his job seriously."

"He's never liked me, though he's not one of my favorite people either."

"You two will learn to get along. But don't worry about that now, because I want you to know I heard you last night, loud and clear." He kissed her on her neck. "Go have fun. We're leaving in a few hours."

Shanice kissed him. "I'll bring you back something."

"I'll have you know, you're taking away the only thing I'm in the mood for. So don't spend too much."

She chuckled and kissed him again as she exited the yacht.

Reaching the dock's parking lot, she immediately called a cab, careful to keep an eye out for a trail during the drive.

"Is that car following us?" she questioned the cab driver.

"The city is compact. Most of the cars take the same roads. That's why there's always traffic here."

She looked in the rearview mirror again. "You can pull over near this building," she ordered.

She paid the driver and exited the vehicle. Keeping up the façade of a tourist taking in a new city, she glanced around and noticed the car trailing her had slowed down. One of the passengers she recognized from the yacht earlier.

Sandoval's men.

She knew he wanted to trust her, and she understood that he couldn't.

I need to lose these guys.

She walked into the closest bar and scanned the room. A middle-aged man looked on as two elderly men played checkers, but it was otherwise empty.

The bar was a mainstay of the town, judging by the décor. The furniture was worn in, and the back of the bar held hundreds of photos of whom she assumed were locals.

Two photos in particular caught her eye, both of which focused on the middle-aged man in the bar. One was a team photo of the Bermudan national baseball team, the bartender front and center. The other was of the same man, a decade older, with what appeared to be his wife, at least ten years younger than him.

She needed to create a distraction, and the photos gave her enough information to create a commotion. She mussed her jet-black curly hair before storming over.

"There you are!" she exclaimed.

"Lady, who are—"

"Where is she?"

"Where is who?"

"Your wife!"

"Nadia?"

"Yeah, Nadia. Where is that homewrecker?"

The man waved Shanice back to the door dismissively. "She's not here, and you shouldn't be either. Come on, you're leaving."

He grabbed for Shanice, but she quickly dodged his grip. "I'm not going anywhere until I beat the ass of the woman who fucked my boyfriend."

The man's eyes widened, and he paused. "Miss, you have to—wait. What did you say?"

"I said, your wife fucked my boyfriend, and I'm here to put my foot in her ass."

The man took a step back in shock and his knees wobbled. "Tell me what you know."

"So, this morning I get up to wash my boyfriend's uniform – he's a decent ball player in the U.S. but couldn't make the big leagues, so he came here because his mother is originally from Bermuda and he was born here, so I guess he can play here on a technicality, but whatever. So—"

"Tell me about my wife!"

"I'm getting to that, sheesh. So, I look at his shirt, and there's this pink lipstick all over the collar—"

"Nadia wears pink lipstick," he gasped, now completely enthralled by Shanice's ruse. ⌐So does every woman!

"So anyway, I confronted him about it and he said it was nothing, that she was just a fan that got a little too close. So I say, 'That explains the smudge on your shirt, now explain the one on the crotch of your pants'. He freezes, so I snatched his phone and ran in the other room and locked the door. I go through his phone and find a video of him and Nadia, giving me all the answers I need."

"Wait, there's a video? L—let me see it."

"I tried to bring it down here because I thought the bitch would deny it, but when I tried to get out of the house, he overpowered me and took his phone back. But I know it's still on there because he's too arrogant to delete proof of his conquests. Oh God, this is Toronto all over again. I can't believe it!" she cried.

It was the performance of a lifetime.

The man, enraged by her words, tried to rest a hand on her shoulder in comfort.

"Don't touch me! For all I know, you're part of this freaky, twisted shit too! I just want answers. Look, here he comes right now, trying to save her."

The man glared at two of Sandoval's men walking across the street towards the bar. He gestured to the other men in the bar to follow him. One of them grabbed a golden bat from the wall and handed it to the bar owner.

"Wait here."

The three men walked out onto the street.

Shanice watched the interaction. The men exchanged heated words until a punch was thrown. It was all she needed to slip her security detail.

She stole a hat and glasses from behind the bar and hailed a taxi headed in the opposite direction. The cab screeched to a halt once she saw the first convenience store, and she ran inside to buy a prepaid burner.

"Omicron, this is Zero."

"Zero, it's Xavion, just where in the hell are you?"

"Bermuda. Where is—"

"Yes! That's perfect. I'm sending you an address. You need to get there as soon as you can."

She hung up the phone as the address came through. She memorized it and threw the phone in a trash can. The location was within walking distance.

When she arrived, she found a powder-blue two-story building that looked to be condemned.

"Carol's Inseams & Alterations," she smirked.

The CIA was almost too clever for its own good.

Shanice walked into the building, not sure what to expect. One thing she was certain of was that whatever Sandoval had planned, it was going down in the next twenty-four hours.

Her heart was conflicted, but her head was clear. She was a soldier, and this was the mission. Even though she cared for him deeply, she had a job to do.

Disarming the security code, she walked into the mostly empty house. Though it seemed abandoned from the outside, the interior was spotless.

Shanice made her way through the house, looking for anything she could use to contact base. Finally, hidden in a closet in a back bedroom, she found a burner cell. She reached for it just as a familiar voice rang through the room.

"You won't be needing that today, Zero."

It was Director Caldwell.

"What in the hell are you doing in Bermuda?"

"It's time we had a talk," he said as he stepped out from the shadows. He held a glass of water, so he'd been sitting there for a while, waiting for her arrival. "Put the phone back in the box and close the closet."

"What are you doing here?"

"I'm verifying that Hal's report is correct. That you are indeed still working for us."

She glared at him. "If you have a problem with the way I'm running this operation, then pull me right now. I'm sure your superiors will forgive you for pulling the only asset who's ever gotten inside of the Seven Syndicate a day before their big plans."

"My superior's concerns are why I'm here. It's been five months and we know nothing of substance about the Algorithm."

"That's because there's nothing to report. The man is very careful with his plans. I spend all of my days—"

"Before you lie to me, remember whose side you're supposed to be on."

"And what does that mean?"

"I find it hard to believe that you spend your days next to the most dangerous terrorist in the world, yet he hasn't given a clue if he's building a bomb or a Lego set."

She threw her hands in the air in frustration. "Look, Caldwell, Sandoval is a genius. His security is next level. There are cameras everywhere. The fact that we're having this conversation is nothing short of a miracle."

"High praise for the man you're trying to capture."

"He's… impressive. To say the least. It would be wrong to underestimate his genius."

Caldwell tilted his head slightly and examined her. "Have you slept with him? Because I'm trying to understand how any of what you just said furthers our mission."

His words, albeit true, offended her. "If I were a man, you wouldn't blink at me having to sleep with a target."

Oop!

"If you were a man, I wouldn't have to wonder if you could emotionally compartmentalize for the sake of the mission. But that's not what this is about, and you know it. Sandoval is charming and, like you said, he's smart. How do you know he isn't playing you?"

His words hit a sore spot. It was a train of thought she didn't want to entertain. "Gee, I don't know, Caldwell. I certainly didn't have a clue when you were playing me."

"What are you talking ab—"

"You sat in that office and fed me a load of crap, 'we know nothing about Sandoval', but what are the odds the most powerful government agency in the world didn't have a clue how the man looked? Makes a person wonder if I got this job because I was good enough, or because I just so happen to look the part."

Caldwell took off his glasses and took a sip from his glass. He sighed. "Okay, all cards on the table. We've never had an agent get this close. We had our suspicions, but we couldn't confirm his identity until you made contact. Hummingbird's attempt at defecting was our first big break in this case, but she wasn't one of ours. So yes, I did have some clue that the man we know as Sandoval was Adonis Carter. We assumed he was an underling at best; we never thought he was the leader of the Syndicate."

he

"I call bullshit."

"You can think whatever you want, Zero. I'm telling you this as a courtesy. Your job is still to find, report, and prevent whatever the

Syndicate has planned. So far, you haven't given me any indication that you can do that."

Her nostrils flared at his words. "I've given you more on the Syndicate in the last five months than you've gotten in the last five years, but that's not your actual issue, is it?"

"What are you talk—"

"I wonder, brotha, which one bugs you more? The fact that a black man could be this many steps ahead of the mighty CIA, or that you need a black woman to catch him for you?" *Wow! Batsy*

Caldwell stepped directly in front of her and looked in her eyes. "For you to even insinuate that this has anything to do with race is offensive. I'll ignore it, because it would make me think less of you, but let me be perfectly clear about the obligations of my job as a Director of the CIA: the only colors I see are red, white, and blue. I'll cut myself and bleed on the damn flag to make sure it stays red. Now, if you have a problem with the manner in which you receive your orders, we can talk about that after the mission. For now, your orders remain as they were: infiltrate the Seven Syndicate and report any useful information to dismantle their operation. Are we clear, Agent Zero?"

"Crystal, sir. Now, let me explain a few of my own expectations," she said, stepping even closer to him. "No more of this on-a-need-to-know bullshit. Shoot straight with me, or not at all. I'm in the field, and it's my ass on the line. The least you can do is give me the intel to help me cover it."

"Fair enough."

The two nodded, accepting their mutual understating.

"From what I can tell, the Algorithm is numerical, but I've never been close enough to see it in action, or even know what I'm looking for. He's concerned only about extremely complex math problems, but I'm not sure for what reason."

"Which means he's not worried about alphanumeric entries. Is he going to rob a bank?"

She dismissed that idea. "Money's not a problem for the Syndicate, so that isn't it."

he's going to take down the entire banking system! money is the root of all evil. Get rid of the have and have nots = level playing field.

"If you had to guess?"

"I'm not sure. Sandoval has electromagnetic pulse generators on the yacht, which shut down any unfamiliar technologies. Here, I stole this phone from his enforcer when he tried to stop me from leaving this morning." She handed him the phone she'd palmed from Bear when he tried to restrain her. "The same is true if this phone doesn't check back in with the server every fifteen minutes."

Caldwell examined it. "This is next-level tech."

"It's virtually useless outside of the range of one of Sandoval's servers. Now that it's off the yacht, the insides are fried. But from what I saw before it died, it seems like they may be headed somewhere in New York... possibly Wall Street."

Caldwell folded his arms and began pacing, processing everything she'd revealed.

"It makes sense, and it's the best intel we got. We're going to set up a tactical team at the pier the moment he steps foot on American soil. I'm on a plane to DC as soon as we're done here to give a detailed report. But it's time to end this. Get this phone back to the yacht. We can't raise any suspicion."

"Keep it. I'm not sure what trackers, GPS, or any other kind of software is installed on it. Besides, I created a distraction to get here, and I'm sure Bear will have bigger things to worry about than a lost phone."

Caldwell nodded and put the phone in his briefcase.

As she was walking past him, she stopped. "Sir, one more thing."

"What's that?"

"If you ever question my professional integrity again, you're gonna have to prove to me why they called you Raven Claw."

Without another word, she walked out of the room.

14

FOR THE CAUSE

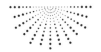

*S*hanice stood on the deck of the yacht. She was conflicted about her job and her love life.

She'd thought they would leave the island the next day, but after the incident with his men, Sandoval moved up his timeline and ordered the crew to leave in the cloak of darkness – giving Caldwell very little time to set up a tactical team. *he didn't say anything to you? Surprised he let you back on the ship*

The closer the yacht moved towards its destination, the more her heart hurt.

It can't end like this.

She watched her lover. Adonis Carter, otherwise known as Sandoval.

She tried to separate the men. Adonis was kind, compassionate, and good-natured, but he'd been playing as Sandoval for so long, she wasn't sure if the two men could be separate anymore.

She glanced back to the water.

After a few hours, her prediction was proving to be right: along the horizon, the torch of the Statue of Liberty started to appear. But the yacht stopped long before it reached the coast.

"Why are we stopping?" Sandoval demanded.

"Sir, I'm afraid the tides won't allow us to bring the yacht in for a few hours."

Sandoval smiled as he walked over to the captain and put his arm on the man's shoulder. "I'm sorry, captain, I'm afraid I know little about the tides. Maybe you can explain something to me?"

"Of course, sir."

"Do the tides own this ship?"

The captain paused before responding. "Er... sir, I'm not sure I understand."

"You said the tides wouldn't allow you to bring the ship in. So I'm asking, do the tides command this ship?"

"No, sir. You do."

"And if I were to have you thrown overboard, would the tide think twice about smashing you against the rocky shore?"

"Uh... no, sir."

"Then maybe you should worry less about the tides, that have no qualms taking your life, and more on me, who's still mulling it over."

"I'll set our course."

"Excuse us for a moment, Captain." Shanice said, interjecting in the conversation.

She pulled Sandoval to the side. "Listen, love. I know you're eager to get to the city, but the captain is right. I grew up around water, and the one thing I learned is to respect the tides."

Sandoval kissed her on her forehead. "I guess we could anchor here for the night. Spend one more night together before the world changes forever?"

"Now you're talking. Come over here and look at the stars with me." She gently grabbed his hand and drew him away.

Sandoval dismissed the captain, and the pair headed to their private room. Shanice tugged at his arm, beckoning him to lie down on the deck and watch the stars.

"Well, I had planned a fancy dinner, but this is nice," Sandoval said.

The two watched the sky, the wind pushing against their bodies.

"There's clarity here, you know? I haven't been this free in a while," Sandoval mused.

"Me either. I can't remember the last time I was just able to look at the sky."

As the waves crashed against the yacht, she made peace with her emotions, still as unsteady as the water below them.

One last night in paradise.

"You see right there? That's Orion's Belt, and over there is the little dipper," he pointed out.

She glanced in the direction he was pointing. "How do you know all of this stuff?"

"I wanted to be an astronomer at one point," he replied. Sandoval smirked as he recalled the memory, looking over at her. "When I was a lad, I loved that show *Deep Space 9*."

"Right, with Avery Brooks."

"It's bloody wicked that you know who Avery Brooks is! Phenomenal actor. I thought his portrayal of Benjamin Sisko was iconic. There was an episode called 'In the Pail of Moonlight.'"

"I remember that one. He did an hour monologue."

"That story just stuck with me."

"How the ends justify the means?"

"It's so simple."

Shanice watched as the wait staff brought *hors d'oeuvres* and drinks for them. They snacked and talked more about the show.

"Enough about me. What did you want to be when you grew up, Mari?"

Shanice lay back against her chair, hands behind her head. "I'm doing it right now."

"You wanted to be a hacker?"

"For as long as I can remember. I mean, it looks and feels a little different to what I'd imagined, but I'm right where I want to be." She winked at him.

Sandoval chuckled. "Oh, I have something for you."

He reached into his pocket and pulled out a small box, handing it to her.

When she opened it, she smiled wide. It was a star necklace, identical to the one she'd broken when she'd first arrived at the villa.

She turned it over and discovered an inscription.

To the brightest Star
And my favorite Kiss
- Sandy GWW

Sandoval stood up and extended his hand to help her up. She faced away so he could clasp the necklace around her neck.

"Just as beautiful as the day I met you."

His words soured the moment. The wall of resistance her mind fought to uphold crumbled.

She was living a lie. The longer it went on, the harder it was to be objective.

She loved his thoughtful nature. Since they'd met, he'd been nothing but accommodating, and she was going to betray his trust.

The assignment had taken its toll on her.

"You don't like it?" Sandoval said.

She schooled her features to show nothing but appreciation for the gift. "I love it. Thank you. You're so incredibly thoughtful."

She wanted to tell him the truth: that the CIA was onto him, and she's been sent to stop him, but how could she? She'd been under-cover for five months, and she still didn't know the plan.

Her team had questioned her loyalty and, if she were being honest with herself, she understood why. There was no question she cared for Sandoval. It would be hard to see him in the hands of the CIA.

She was remorseful, knowing that tonight would be their last night together. The CIA was preparing for their arrival, despite not being sure of the Syndicate's plan.

She fantasized about getting arrested with Sandoval and maintaining her cover in case they needed her later. But she knew there would be no such reprieve with the CIA. She just didn't want to hurt the man who'd cared for her so much.

Better than a bullet in the head. This is definitely a test

She'd made the mistake of getting too close.

She wanted a life with him. But that meant not only the end of civilization as she knew it, but also the end of a career she'd worked her entire life for. A career that had already cost her her current life.

She thought about all she'd sacrificed to join the Agency. Her impeccable Army career, her relationship with her best friend Trina – who she was certain was a complete wreck when she'd heard of her death – and it also cost her the chance at a life with Marcus.

"Winters..." she muttered.

"Hm?"

"Oh, I was just thinking how I love winters here," she said.

Another lie.

It was the first time she'd thought about Marcus since Caldwell made her choose between saving Marcus' life and joining the CIA.

You've come too far now to throw it all away. It's already cost you too much.

She stood up to look over the edge of the yacht, Sandoval close behind. He wrapped his arms around her and kissed her neck. She squeezed his arms, pressing them tightly to her body.

"What's wrong, love?"

She closed her eyes, making one last attempt to help him. "Adonis, what if none of this had to happen?"

"What do you mean?"

"I mean, what if we just ran away together?" She turned to grab both of his hands, looking deep into his dark brown eyes. "What if we forget about it all? Just focus on us. Build a life just for the two of us."

His hand stroked her face gently before he turned his back to her, looking over the water. "When I'm done with this world, we won't ever need to run again."

She tried again, more insistent. "You don't have to do this, Adonis. I know you think you need to, but you don't."

He sighed. "There are times I think that all of this has gone too far, that I don't want to do any of this. Maybe I should settle down, have a family, raise talented children, watch them grow old with the woman I love – with you. But then I think, what kind of world am I bringing a family into? A world where billionaires let the poor starve, knowing damn well they can never spend the amount of money they've made? The same billionaires that underpay their employees so much they have to choose between eating that week or paying their bills. Where companies pour chemicals into drinking water so those same companies can make money on fixing the problem they created. A world where you can be murdered for looking like us.

"This world is a nightmare that needs fixing. I'd be bringing my kids into a world they'd have to fix. That's not a world I want anyone to live in."

She understood his passion; it was something she'd admired since she'd met him.

Sandoval turned around and looked directly in her eyes. "I'm not afraid of dying, Mari. They killed Martin for being nonviolent, and Malcolm for defending himself. All the good they did, death still came for them both. When I was young I didn't understand why, but as I grew up, I realized the system was their real enemy. The system is no different from a homeless man bullying a kid too scared to fight back, and I can't ignore it, because at the end of the day, I'm always gonna be that kid with the brick in my hand."

"Just because you have the brick, doesn't mean you have to throw it, Adonis."

A tear fell across his cheek. "Yes, it does. That's who I am, who I'll always be, and if I die being that person, then I lived a good life."

Her eyes welled. She respected him so much, but she knew she had to let him go in order to do her job.

He kissed her furiously, leading her back to their room for their most intimate love session yet, as if both knowing it would be their last time.

She was ready, willing, and eager to please him. She pushed him onto the bed and kissed his muscular body, from his neck down his torso. His dick quickly hardened.

She drew his dick between her full lips, letting the combination of precum and saliva trickle out the side of her mouth.

"Damn, that's bloody good," he moaned.

She licked his shaft, then she sat up and climbed on top of him, gracefully rocking until he began to thrust inside of her.

He sat up and locked eyes with her as she rode him to ecstasy, grinding her pussy on his pulsating dick and saturating him with her juices.

"I'm cumming! Oh God," he moaned, and an explosion of heat and moisture filled her body, making her even wetter as he slid in and out of her. The thought of his cum spilling inside of her pussy turned her on, to the point she began to reach her own orgasm as she bounced on his still-hard dick.

"Oh my god," she moaned.

Exhausted, she fell onto his chiseled chest into a deep sleep.

She woke up right before dawn and hopped into the shower, ready to prepare for the day, having gotten the closure she needed.

She stepped out of the bathroom and walked over to the bed, realizing that Sandoval was nowhere to be seen.

"Sandy?" she called.

There was no answer.

She dressed and walked outside and down the hall. She didn't see Bear either. In fact, nobody was around.

She felt a sinking feeling in the pit of her stomach.

"You've gotta be kidding me," she uttered as she realized the boat was empty.

Are they gonna come back or did he abandon you?

15

SOLITUDE VIVIFIES; ISOLATION KILLS

"*S*andoval?"

After looking all over the ship and finding nobody on board, she'd reached the deck.

The wine bottle from last night caught her eye.

A memory suddenly came back to her: Sandoval insisting on one last drink.

Walking over, she peered inside the bottle. As she'd suspected: a small amount of white residue sat on the lip of the bottle.

He'd wanted her unconscious while he went into the city to enact his plans.

He was always one step ahead of everyone, including her.

"I've got to quit getting drugged," she huffed.

Omicron needed to be contacted. She could steer the yacht if necessary, so she wasn't stranded, but losing sight of the target the day before his plans was definitely something the team needed to know.

She walked towards the bridge to the captain's desk. She examined the maritime equipment, looking at the console for the emergency mini boats. They had deployed three of the four boats. That was her way back to the mainland.

If anybody was still on the yacht, they'd be close by guarding the remaining boat.

She headed to the bottom floor of the yacht, toward the kitchen.

There were three men standing in the hall talking to each other.

Shanice crept back up the stairs and closed the cabin door, sealing the kitchen off. She turned on all the gas stoves and waited for the fumes to build. She grabbed a knife and secured it in her back pocket before heading back down the stairs.

"Ms. Patterson, I'm sorry, I was supposed to be on the main deck when you woke up."

"Where is Sandoval?"

"He's gone. He told me to tell you that he'd be back."

Shanice glanced at the one remaining mini boat, assessing her options. She knew she could take the guard's gun, but couldn't risk a shootout.

She addressed the closest man. "I was wondering if you could help me with something?"

"Sure, what do you nee—"

Before he could finish, she'd stabbed him in the neck, falling to the ground.

The other two guards jumped up and pulled their weapons as she ran up the stairs to the kitchen, closely followed by the guards, their guns pointed at her.

She raised her hands in surrender. "This room is filling with gas. If you shoot, we all die."

The guards could see she wasn't bluffing.

They put their guns away.

The first guard rushed Shanice. He tried to grab her, but she picked up a pan hanging from a hook overhead and hit him directly in the face, collapsing to the ground. She bashed the pan against his skull a second time for good measure, knocking him out.

The second guard tried to tackle her. Before he could get close, she threw a pan at him with her free hand, giving her time to reposition herself near the knives. She picked up a chef's knife and gripped it tightly.

The man stopped in his tracks, moving into a tactical stance. "Who are you?" he wondered, clearly surprised by her skill.

She grabbed another knife and rushed him. The man dodged several of her swings until she threw one of the knives at him, lodging it in his shoulder.

The guard stumbled backwards, giving Shanice the opening to slit his throat.

As he held his hands to his throat in a futile effort to stop the blood flow, she took the same knife and threw it at the guard that had started getting up. Catching him in the chest, he fell to the ground holding his chest.

She walked over to him and took off his mask. "You're losing a lot of blood, but I'll let you live if you tell me where Sandoval is."

"Screw you."

She grabbed another knife and chopped off his pinky finger.

The man howled in pain.

"Now you're losing even more blood. First your fingers, then your toes. You have nineteen more chances. Where is Sandoval?"

The man hesitated, and Shanice lifted the knife to cut another finger off when the man muttered, "He's going to the United Nations."

She stood up and stepped on the knife in his chest, killing him instantly. Vicious.

She took his phone and headed toward the last mini boat. The phone wouldn't work once she left the yacht. She headed to the deployment console to ready the boat while she called her team.

"Omicron, this is Zero. I've lost eyes on the target. Where is the tactical team?"

"Zero, this is Caldwell. We've been trying to get in touch with them for hours, but we've heard nothing. Where is Sandoval?"

"He drugged me and left in the middle of the night. When I woke up, it was just me with three guards on the boat."

"How many people traveled on the boat?"

"Almost twenty. I'm heading to shore now. Do we know about anything significant going on in New York today?"

"Nothing of significance on Wall Street. There was an

international meeting at the United Nations, but with the prime minister of Turks and Caicos being poisoned this morning, we—"

"Wait, what? Back up. What happened?"

"You don't know?"

"What happened?"

"The prime minister was supposed to meet at the United Nations today to sign a treaty to help trade with some of the smaller nations. Our working theory is that one of Sandoval's men poisoned him before he got on the plane."

"What about the villa?"

"Well, once the prime minister was down, we requested through not-so-diplomatic channels that we take the lead on searching the villa. It was empty."

"What do you mean, it's empty?"

"There was no staff, no power, no devices. Someone wiped the villa clean."

"That doesn't make sense. What happened to everybody?"

"Our assumption is that everybody at the villa got on a boat, along with whatever data Sandoval may have left behind. But that's small potatoes; about an hour ago, each of the yachts exploded in the middle of the ocean. All except the one you were on."

"All six yachts exploded?" she repeated, stunned by the news.

"We sent a team to investigate some of the debris that's made its way into international waters. There's a good chance everyone was already dead before the explosion." — staff that would talk. He was tricky them not FBI

"Zero, this is Xavion. We ran forensics on a few of the bodies we recovered. Their lungs were filled with carbon monoxide."

"He killed his own people, his followers. In one move, he killed everyone that could talk about the Algorithm."

"If nothing else, he's efficient. What's your ETA to the mainland?"

She finished deploying the boat and jumped in. "I'm on my way there now. Sandoval is going to the U.N. Send a tactical team there immediately!"

91

16

OMICRON

"*I* only have myself to blame," she muttered into the wind, the sound of the mini engine drowning out the noise as she sped towards the coastline of New York City. Sleeping with the target was one thing, but allowing him to escape was entirely different.

"Fuck!" she yelled as she shook her head.

How could I let my guard down this much?

She pushed the thought from her mind. Of all the things that had happened today, guilt was a low priority. There were more important things to worry about.

When she got to the shore, she immediately looked for a cell phone. She managed to palm one from a couple walking with a pram. *stroller*

She walked a few paces and called headquarters. "Omicron, this is Zero."

"Zero this is Caldwell. Where are you?"

"I'm on the docks. Where's your tactical team?"

"Our team should've been there hours ago." Caldwell replied.

Shanice looked around the pier for anything out of the ordinary. Up ahead, a bin had been overturned, and a few dark splatters were on the ground.

"Hold on, Omicron, I may have found something."

She followed the trail of blood to a nearby shed, forcing it open to look around.

The trail of blood stopped in the corner of the room, beyond a pile of oars.

She threw the oars to the side, revealing a dead body. "Omicron, tactical team is down. I repeat, the tactical team is down."

"What is happ—"

She hung up the phone. There was no time to lose.

Transportation in the area was scarce, making it difficult to get into the city.

"Damn it!" she yelled out loud.

Her vulnerability had caused her to lose sight of the mission. She was furious with herself. Her feelings for the man couldn't take precedent to the innocent lives he was about to take.

She sprinted up the dock and scanned again for a vehicle, spotting a man getting off a jet-black Kawasaki motorcycle. She sprinted over to the guy and tapped him on the shoulder.

"I'm so sorry about this."

She punched him in the face and knocked him out cold, taking his keys.

She jumped on the bike and revved the engine, speeding toward the United Nations plaza.

Time was not on her side.

She drove as fast as she could, cutting down one-way streets, swerving through oncoming traffic as she headed towards her destination. The light turned red when she was just a block away. She sped through the red light, almost getting hit by an 18-wheeler in the process.

"Shit!"

She continued to speed towards her destination.

Once she'd arrived at the plaza, she jumped off the motorcycle and called Omicron base.

Director Caldwell picked up. "Agent Zero, we ran several U.N.

guests through face recognition. See if you recognize any of them. Xavion is sending them to your phone now."

She scanned the images as they came in. The effort felt futile until she saw a face she recognized. "The last one. That's Bear! Sandoval's enforcer, he's with a man I saw in Turks a few months ago."

"That's the former Russian ambassador, Sergi Yousolf. He was excommunicated from the Kremlin three days ago."

"He must have given Sandoval access to the Russian detail."

"Okay, I'll reach out to the Russians to see what their business is with—"

"There's no time for that. Whether they're involved or not, they will almost certainly deny it, and whatever Sandoval is planning will be happening in the next few minutes. We have to do something now!"

"Zero, the United Nations is intentional territory. No country can just walk on the premises without authoriza—"

"I gotta go, Caldwell."

Shanice spotted her way into the building: a catering truck pulling onto the road leading to the back entrance of the plaza.

She pulled in front of the car and stopped the bike.

The truck stopped, and the driver got out. "What's the matter?"

"I don't know, it just stalled."

"Well, let me see if—"

Before he could respond, Shanice slammed his head against the front of his truck, knocking him unconscious. She dragged him into the bushes, stripping him of his business shirt. Taking control of his truck, she drove through the security checkpoints, determined to stop the man she loved.

17
THE UNITED NATIONS

parked?

She packed the truck in the loading dock, rid herself of the borrowed shirt and walked through the kitchen. She swiped a knife from a bench, looking for a trace of the Syndicate.

Come on, Gib, think.

She didn't have a clue where they would be, and didn't know where to start. She needed to come up with a plan. She scanned the workers in the kitchen.

Adonis is a man of the people. He would've talked to someone who had a lowly job.

It was a shot in the dark, but she was out of options.

She pulled out the phone she'd stolen earlier and pulled up the picture of Bear. She showed his picture to the staff, but no one had seen him.

She moved into a hallway that led to the main area. There were at least a dozen doors, all leading somewhere else in the building. "I gotta narrow this down."

An idea struck her.

She went to the fire alarm and pulled it, scanning the hallway.

Within moments, people flooded the hallway from all directions, except one.

"The boiler room."

She spotted two men disguised as plumbers standing by the boiler room door.

Neither of them budged.

Shanice walked toward them. As she drew closer, one of the men looked at her in shock; he must have recognized her from the villa. He was about to reach for his pistol when she rushed him, stabbing him in the abdomen and grabbing his gun before his body hit the ground.

Before he could react, she turned toward the second man and shot him in the head. *hope these guys reallyarent CIA agents*

The crowd began to scream and run from the sound of the gunshots, and another siren rang in concert with the fire alarm.

She opened the boiler room door and went inside.

The entrance held nothing but a dead janitor.

Stepping over him, Shanice walked further through the rooms. There were large water heaters along the railed hallways, washing machines on the lower level.

Attached to the heating structures were the metal plates Sandoval had created. He had rigged the entire heating structure.

"With all the natural gas flowing through this building, it's going to be a pile of rubble."

Before she could act, a voice echoed down the hallway. "That's the last one. Now we can get out of here."

There were two men, along with Sandoval and Bear.

She stepped out of the shadows. "Adonis Carter, stop what you're doing. You're under arrest."

Sandoval stopped, confused by the words, and turned to face her. "Mari? What are you doing?"

"Don't move, Sandy. Please don't make this any harder than it already is."

"I don't understand. Why would you do this?"

He seemed genuinely confused by what was going on.

"I need you to drop your weapons and disable these bombs."

"I was building a world for you!" he bellowed.

A tear fell from Shanice's eye as she replied. "Sandy... you're about to blow up the United Nations. That's not a world I want to live in."

its just a building! Everyone got out because you pulled fire alarm—remember

Sandoval paced back and forth, unsure what to do.

One of his men addressed him. "Sir, we have to go now."

Sandoval pulled out a gun and shot him in the head. He turned back to Shanice. "I'm going to leave now, Mari. If my men or I see you again, we will kill you."

He turned to his men and said, "Now we can leave."

"I'd like to stay."

Sandoval stopped and looked at Bear. "You know, the devices work on the same principle as our other devices." *?*

"I'll be out of here before you get far enough away to detonate them."

Sandoval and Bear touched their foreheads together, then the two men walked out the door.

Shanice watched as Bear trained his gun on her, and she mirrored him. "I knew you were a mole. I felt it in my bones."

"You've been wanting a piece of me since we've met. Well, come on, big boy. Ain't nothing between us but air and opportunity. Let's dance."

Shanice slowly lowered her weapon at the same time as Bear.

Once both weapons were on the ground, Shanice raised her arms and took two steps in his direction. Bear, fearless as usual, took four steps. *how?.*

She threw the knife she'd from the yacht into his shoulder and, before he could react, she picked up her pistol and shot him three times, forcing him over the railing and onto one of the industrial washing machines.

touché

"Who says you shouldn't bring a knife to a gunfight?" she mocked as she glanced over at the body lying on top of the washer. Blood pooled around his head.

She walked over and grabbed his gun before stepping up to study the bomb. It's only distinguishing feature was the number '7' on the front.

This building needed to be evacuated *now*.

She ran through the door that Sandoval had exited. It led to the loading dock.

She ran at full speed to the front of the building.

A guard up ahead saw her approaching and yelled, "Drop the gun now!"

Shanice raised her hands in surrender. "Listen to me. I'm a federal agent. We have to—"

"I said, don't move."

"I'm not moving, okay? We have to get everybody away from the building! There's a bomb inside!"

The guard came over and secured her, placing her in handcuffs.

"Listen to me! I work for the U.S. government, and I'm telling you, there is a bomb in the—"

Kaboom!

She felt the heat before the force of the explosion threw her ten feet away.

Sou couyant — forged in the fire

18
WHEN IT ALL FALLS DOWN

reathe, just breathe.

Shanice fought through the smoke and ash to fill her lungs with oxygen. She coughed violently as she gasped for air.

There were first responders everywhere.

Her mind went back to her parents, and 9/11 – how they must have felt in their last moments. It was all too much.

She was feeling the full weight of her failure. She'd joined the Agency in the hopes of one day preventing something as catastrophic as what had happened to her parents. But instead, she was now enduring a similar attack.

A guard came up to her as she sat in the back of an ambulance. "We were able to stop five of the seven bombs. Only fifteen casualties."

"That's good."

"Also, there's a phone call for you."

The soldier handed her a phone. She knew who it was, and she knew he'd be upset.

"Director Caldwell, sir, I—"

"Before we begin, how are you feeling?"

"I'm fine... I just—"

"Good, now that I know you're fine, I can begin. I hired you for your discretion. I hired you to protect our country, and your first course of action was to charge headfirst into what is now an international and diplomatic clusterfuck. I needed a scalpel, not a sword, and you showed up like a goddamn machete."

"Caldwell, I get that you're upset, but I'm telling you, this isn't over. Sandoval never does anything that he doesn't in some way feel can benefit the people. This attack on the U.N. isn't his end game."

"But it is yours, Agent Zero. Your assignment is over. How you found yourself to be directly involved in one of the biggest terrorist acts on American soil since 9/11 on your first assignment is beyond me. I'm ordering you back to Langley for debriefing. The pentagon is demanding we turn over all intel we have on Sandoval."

Shanice looked at the people around here, hurt and bleeding.

She'd let her guard down, and it had cost lives. She had to make this right.

"Caldwell, you can't do this."

"We trusted you, and you let us down, Agent Zero. As of this moment, you're to stand down. Report back to Langley and give them everything you know."

"Sir, listen to me. I know Sandoval. The U.N. was not the main act. He has a larger plan—"

"Agent Zero, my patience with you is ice-thin. I can't afford to spend another—"

"With all due respect, sir, you've been tracking the Seven Syndicate for years. I've given you the leader – hell, the entire Syndicate on a silver platter in under six months. I need to see this through."

"Agent Zero, my decision is fina—"

Click.

She hung up. There was no way she could let this assignment go. Sandoval was on the loose. There had to have been something she missed.

She thought back on her time with Sandoval. His smile, their endless discussions, his complete trust in her.

She recalled dancing to Sade, and his tender touch.

She thought about his face when he'd discovered she was undercover.

She knew Adonis Carter, and she knew Sandoval. Both of them had a singular focus.

"I know what he plans on doing."

She walked back up the street to where she'd left the motorcycle and called Omicron.

Director Caldwell answered. "Agent Zero, I told you to head back to—"

"Shut up and listen. Sandoval is too damn smart for the U.N. to be his ultimate play. Think about it: why would he go through all this trouble of working on the Algorithm? We still don't know what it's about, but he's using it to blow up a building with minor casualties?"

"If by 'minor casualties' you mean killing one world leader and critically injuring at least a dozen more, causing an international incident, then yes, I would say he accomplished this minor task. I've been told that my dry humor can be lost on some people, so to be clear, I'm joking, and I hope you are too."

"I'm not joking. There's something bigger going on, and I know you don't trust me right now, but you hired me to do a job, and I'm going to do it. If you want to stop me, track my location and, when you find me, put a bullet in both of us, but I'm going after Sandoval."

The director was silent. After a few minutes, he said, "Forget what you can prove. Tell me, what's your theory?"

Shanice arrived at the motorcycle. "The Seven Syndicate is all about creating a new world order."

"Right, and if his plan was successful, all governments of the world would be crippled."

"Right, but he doesn't care about power, not in that way. He wants to bring down the system. What happens when the U.N. is attacked?"

"The Geneva Convention requires all countries to immediately send relief money to the U.N."

"That's it! It's the money."

"I thought you said he didn't care about money."

"He doesn't, but the rest of the world does. Listen, whatever the

Algorithm is, I know it's a complex numerical virus. I think Sandoval wanted this attack to be big and messy, so the governments of the world would unite and send funds to one location."

"In an attempt to do what?"

"I think whatever this thing does, it somehow destroys the financial systems of the world governments."

"Stand by, Zero," Caldwell ordered.

Shanice continued to ride out of the city. After a few moments, Xavion joined them on the phone.

"Zero, I think you might be right. From what I can tell, our role in this was to create a subroutine that forced a number higher or lower than the answer input. For example, one plus one is two, but the hack I designed will change that answer to whatever the user wants. I think this virus is programmed to forcibly delete any numerical data. I thought it was weird at first, but now it makes sense."

"What does that mean?" she asked.

"If you're right, it means that whenever someone connects to a terminal, the virus will spread, and force every figure to be whatever Sandoval wants."

"Seven."

"If that's what he wants."

She thought about his words. Suddenly she fully understood his plan.

"Guys, listen to me. Sandoval is going to wipe out all monetary values permanently! The moment any government sends funds to the U.N., the virus will infect not only the U.N. banking system but every government — every bank in the world's financial system, changing all financial values down the number 7. He'll reset the playing field for the world. Caldwell, you have to go to the Secretary of State and let them know that the world's financial systems are in jeopardy."

"It's too late. About 90 percent of the countries have already sent a relief package of some kind, including the U.S. It's all going to a central U.N. account."

"Then we have to assume he already has access to the world's financial systems," she said. "He's going to need a large server farm to process this much data, and that will take time to execute. Can you find any large spikes in energy use or heat signatures within a forty mile radius of here?"

There was a brief``````` pause and then Xavion said, "A massive spike on the electric grid came through Canada's energy system about fifteen minutes ago."

"Then that's where he is. Caldwell, how soon can we get a tactical team there?"

[handwritten: Say she is going to the power plant At]

"We can't. For one thing, all our resources are at the U.N. assisting with securing the world leaders – not to mention it's on the other side of the U.S./Canadian border. With Canada being an ally, we can't risk having a spy getting caught on foreign soil. I'll inform the Canadian prime minister that—"

"There isn't time for that. Sandoval has been three steps ahead of us this whole time. He knows the level of red tape this is going to involve. His plan is happening now! Listen to me, Caldwell. My job is to not get caught on international soil. Trust me to do this."

There was a silence, but after a spell, Caldwell said, "Then you're our only hope, Agent Zero. Track down Sandoval and stop him, at any cost. I don't have to emphasize to you the gravity of this situation. The fate of the world as we know it is in your hands."

Shanice revved the motorcycle and sped off towards the Canadian border, filled with purpose.

I only hope I'm not too late.

[handwritten: from NYC?! You are going to hit traffic on the FDR lol. E 42nd → Canada ~8hr drive or ~2hr flight]

19
BEWARE THE STRANGER

how didja know where to go?

"*T*his is it," she mumbled as she pulled up to the compound.

It was now nightfall; she'd ridden nonstop to get here in time to stop Sandoval. The odds were against her, but the Army trained her to fight under these conditions.

She got off the bike, climbed the fence and moved to find cover using a nearby tree. Moving in the shadows was easy for her.

Shanice checked her ammo. Four bullets left, but that wasn't a concern right now. She thrived in hand-to-hand combat and relished in the direct approach.

Time to be the scalpel... for Bravo.

She moved like the night's wind.

As far back as childhood, she had been credited with moving like a ghost. She'd often terrified her childhood friends by disappearing and reappearing out of nowhere.

Her dark skin only added to the camouflage her black cat suit provided. She scanned for a patrolman – one was taking a cigarette break away from his post.

"*Perfect.*"

She needed more ammo, and he was in the ideal position to be ambushed. She crept behind him slowly, blending in with the shadows. She was two feet behind him when he felt her presence, but before he could react, she rushed him and pressed the gun directly against his abdomen.

Thump, thump!

The sound of the gunshot was muffled by the gun being pressed directly against him. He fell to the ground instantly, his body hitting the concrete.

She took his weapon, tactical gear, and his phone. She'd just hidden the body next to a tree when she heard another guard walking the route. Shanice took cover behind the tree and held still.

The guard was walking towards the area where the first guard was killed.

Can't risk a shootout. From this distance, the gunshots would be too loud.

She searched the body of the first guard again and found a silencer. "Sweet black Jesus, thank you!"

She secured the silencer and waited for the guard, who was now inspecting the area. She watched him lean toward the ground.

Damn, he sees the blood.

She stepped out of the shadows again and shot him.

Thump! Thump!

The guard fell to the ground.

That should be all the guards on this side.

She didn't bother to hide the body. One thing she'd learned while living in the villa was the patrol routine of Sandoval's men. They worked two per quadrant to secure the building.

"I've got two minutes."

She set her watch for a minute and forty-five seconds and sprinted to the next quadrant. She saw the next guard and snuck up behind him. She took out the stolen tactical knife and sliced the guard's throat before he even knew what was happening.

She then rushed, pistol in hand, and quickly found the next guard.

Thump!

She killed him with a head shot with her silenced pistol. She continued to move toward the main building.

Suddenly, she heard the chirp of the walkie talkie. "Section two, report."

Damn it, they're early.

She was out of time; it was now or never.

Taking the mask off the first guard, she sprinted over to the edge of the lake directly in front of the compound, avoiding detection. She stuffed two grenades inside the mask and pulled the pins halfway out.

As the remaining guards zeroed in on her position, she scurried down to the edge of the lake and got in the water. As she heard the guards get closer, she counted.

There were about a half dozen men.

She took a deep breath and submerged herself in the water.

5...4...3...2...

Kaboom!

Shanice emerged from the water, gun in hand, and scanned the area. The explosion had taken out four of the six guards. Two of them were still on the ground, recovering from the explosion. She made light work of them, killing them both.

That's all the perimeter guards. Let's see what's waiting for me on the inside.

Shanice walked towards a hole in the wall made by the explosion. She'd be walking into an ambush if she went through the hole.

She rushed back over to the dead guards' bodies and took four grenades from them. Why would they be carrying grenades grand

With the stealth of a jaguar hunting its prey, she crept near the edge of the wall, now crumbling thanks to the first explosion. a power plant?

She took two grenades and pulled the pins, throwing them as far as she could along the side of the wall.

Kaboom!

The multiple explosions shook the foundation of the wall, causing the south side to collapse, which was all the distraction she needed. She entered the building through the first hole and killed two soldiers with ease. She tried to find cover when a bullet grazed her left bicep.

"Damn it!" she cursed as she regrouped behind a wall of computer stations. She searched for the remaining guards. One tried to charge around the corner, and she killed him instantly. Another guard tried to sneak up on her from the second floor. She shot him twice in the chest, his body falling over the balcony.

One more.

She moved from her position. The guard shot at her as she dove behind another rack of servers, the bullets destroying it. She pulled the pin on the grenade and rolled it toward the guard.

Kaboom.

The guard managed to get out of the way, but she had her gun trained on him.

Thump! Thump!

She killed him instantly.

There was only one person left to face.

"That's far enough, Mari," Sandoval called out.

She stepped out into the open.

Sandoval was there, holding a gun aimed at her.

"Adonis, it's over. It won't be long before the Canadian military arrives."

"You think that's going to stop me? Please, the Algorithm is already making its way behind every firewall in the world. In fifteen minutes, the only number anyone will see is the number 7. Currency will be meaningless."

She saw the hurt in his eyes, her betrayal like rubbing alcohol on an open wound. The last thread was pulled in her web of lies and deceit.

Sandoval looked at the ground. She could tell he was deep in thought. After a spell, he laughed – first slowly, then a louder roar. "I'm sorry. I'm just laughing at the bloody irony of it all. Helpless, innocent Mari Patterson killed twelve of the most hardened mercenaries I could afford. I always said you made me feel like Samson, and know I know why, Delilah. I can't understand why I didn't see it. I was able to dodge MI-6, the CIA, and the KGB for six years. A kid from nowhere with nothing, staying one step ahead of the smartest minds in the world. I thought of every countermeasure, except when it came

107

to my heart. My goddamn heart that, even despite this betrayal, is still very much in love with you."

"Sandy, you don't love me. You don't know me."

"Don't do that! I know four different ways to make you cum in under ten minutes."

"Yes, you can satisfy me physically, but you still don't know me. I was playing a role."

"Hogwash! I know you like no other." he yelled as he waved the gun in the air. He looked at her and a tear fell from his eyes. "You like Jamaican-blend coffee, two creams, two sugars. If you could eat only one thing in the world, it would be your mom's johnny cake, and you think the Thundercats reboot is taking entirely too long to come to TV. Lie to yourself, but you can't lie to me."

lol

She tried to block out his words, but there was truth in every one of them.

She met his eyes as he continued. "I looked in your eyes and watched you call my name. You couldn't fake the look in your eyes when I was inside you. How you allowed me to make you feel. I know you love me, and now I know why you struggled to say it."

"Adonis, my job is to stop—"

"To bloody hell with your job. We had everything! We had each other!" he yelled. As he fixed the gun on her, he shook his head.

"Cut the shit, Adonis! I know what happened on the other yachts. You were going to do the same thing to me!"

Sandoval jostled the gun in his hand. "I was always coming back for you. It hurts that you still don't believe that. But not as much as the fact that you've been lying to me since the day we met. I've been playing it over and over in my head. I can't believe last night on the yacht meant nothing to you."

"If it meant something to you, then stop this."

"You know what I don't understand: why? There was no part of me that wasn't accessible. I was building a world for you to rule, and it wasn't enough." *You were not doing this for her! She never asked for*

"No one wants to be queen of a pile of corpses, Adonis." *this. You had this planned ahead*

Sandoval nodded, and she watched a teardrop fall to his cheek. "If *ea or of time* you don't want to rule the corpses, then maybe you'd prefer living with the fact that you just made one."

He walked out of the room and returned with a beaten and bloodied man wearing a black hood over his head.

Sandoval removed the hood.

"Hal!"

Shanice pointed the gun at Sandoval and yelled, "Hal! Are you okay?"

Sandoval chuckled. "I'm sorry. Do you two know each other? That's funny, because at the market the other day, you said he was just a stranger."

"Hal, talk to me!" she shouted, still aiming the gun at Sandoval.

"Been better kid… now shoot him," Hal pleaded.

Adonis hit him in the back of the head with the pistol, causing him to stumble to his knees.

"Hal!" she yelled.

Sandoval glared at her. "You see, I thought something was off with this bloke the moment I saw him. I thought he was using you to get to me. Never did I once imagine the two of you were working together. We've tortured him for days, and not one word about it. I guess there's something to be said for CIA training."

"Let him go, Sandy!"

"That's who you're working for, right?"

"Adonis…"

"Answer me!"

Shanice was silent. She never took her eyes off Sandoval, but she couldn't deny it. In this moment, there was no more place for lies.

He shook his head. "I know how to get the answers I need. See, I know you love me, and I know those government agencies brainwash you with all their rhetoric, so we're going to do a double-blind experiment."

"Sandy, put the gun do— "

"It's time to prove what you love more."

"Sandy, you need to—"

"I'm going to kill this man in five seconds, or you're going to kill me." *oh! Time to Choose!*

"Adonis!"

"Love or loyalty, which one will you choose?" Adonis pulled Hal to a standing position and put the gun to his head.

"Five."

"Adonis, you don't have to do th—"

"Four."

"Sandy, please just listen to m—"

"Three."

Shanice lifted her gun. "If you kill him, you'll be the next person in line at the gates."

"Two."

"Hal, are you good?"

"What are you waiting for, kid? Do it already!" Hal yelled.

"One."

Pop! Pop!

20

SANDY AND MARI

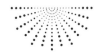

*H*er bullet went through Hal's shoulder into Sandoval's. He dropped the gun and fell in agony. Shanice rushed over to the pair and kicked the gun out of reach, then turned to Hal. "Are you alright?"

"Been better. Good work, kid." He groaned as he collapsed on the ground.

Shanice helped him sit up. "Can you make it out of here?"

Hal nodded in agreement. She took the phone she'd taken earlier and handed it to him. "Give Omicron our status. I'm going to try to shut this thing down."

Hal agreed and limped out of the building as fast as he could to make the call.

Shanice turned to Sandoval, who was still on the floor bleeding from his shoulder.

She walked over and kneeled on his wound. Sandoval screamed in frustration. "I don't even know your real name."

"It doesn't matter now. It's over."

"Was any of it real to you?" he asked.

Shanice thought back to the moment they met: his smile and

Aww

sincerity. He'd loved her like he didn't know how to stop. Earning her heart, her trust, her faith in him, and it was all built on a lie.

She locked eyes with him, recalling their time together in a world built on a complicated illusion of deceptions that began long before either of them met.

She knew he was hurting. She also knew he needed honesty.

She touched the necklace he gave her. "It was... all of it was."

The two shared a kiss, one that felt like goodbye. When he pulled away, she said. "Adonis. I love you, but I've learned I love my job more. You don't know what it's already cost... what it's still costing me. I absolutely need this."

He said nothing, stunned by her actions. He looked her in the eyes.

She put the gun underneath his chin. "Give me the code, Adonis. Now."

Still he said nothing. She looked at him pleadingly. "Please don't make me kill you."

The blood poured from his shoulder. She looked into his eyes – there was nothing. Emptiness replaced his passion.

She pulled the gun away from his chin and stood up.

"Damn it."

Suddenly, she heard a phone ring. She walked over to pick it up. "Yeah?"

"Zero, this is Hal. I got in touch with Omicron. The Canadian military is sending a drone to destroy the compound. ETA is under two minutes." *Why would you blow everything up?*

"Copy that."

She turned back to Sandoval. "Adonis... Look, I know you don't want to die. What you're trying to do is going to create a lot more tyrants than it will good men like you. Please, just give me the code."

Sandoval sat up and took a deep breath and looked into her eyes. "The code is us. It's always been us."

Shanice thought about his words, touching the necklace he'd given her. She stood up and rushed over to the terminal, moving through the debris, which had caught aflame, and made her way to the console to put in the abort code. The clock was ticking, and there was no more time to waste. She typed in what she hoped was the code.

SandyandMari

The console froze. One pillar fell onto the ground, the fire now spreading. Her eyes watered from the smoke as she stood at the console.

"Come on, damn it."

It wouldn't have mattered if the building was destroyed if the virus wasn't manually stopped.

Code incorrect.

"Damn it! She tried another code.

SandovalandStarkiss69

The computer froze again. A minute passed. She was low on time.

"Come on… come on," she muttered.

After a few moments, the computer came back.

Code accepted - would you like to abort?

"Yes!" she yelled as she entered the word into the computer.

Upload terminated.

Kaboom!

She turned around to see the room consumed with fire.

"Adonis!" she yelled. There was no answer, and now there was no time – the drone would be there in moments.

Still, she tried to get to him, but the fire was raging too large. One of the server towers fell, blocking her path towards him.

Suddenly, the phone rang again.

"The code was accepted. I'm trying to get Sand—"

"Kid, get the hell out of there now!"

Shanice bolted toward the door. She had to kick it twice to open it. Finally it sprung open and she sprinted as fast as possible.

She looked up and saw the drone within striking distance. There was nowhere for her to run. As the missile launched, she ran toward the lake and dove into the water.

Kaboom.

The entire compound began to crumble. Shards of glass and flaming debris hit the water.

She didn't see him — maybe he got out while she was typing?

She held her breath for as long as she could while swimming away from the explosion. Finally, she came up for air and coughed violently as a mixture of smoke, water, and oxygen filled her lungs.

She was safe. But Sandoval, who had already been bleeding and unable to move, was killed in the explosion. *Sure abart that?*

She heard the sirens of the Canadian police approaching.

As she continued to swim to shore, she thought of her lover.

She was still in the water – the place she went to grieve her parents. The only place she'd ever felt safe.

No one could hear her screams or see her tears. She stuck her head underwater and grieved her fallen lover.

2 1

THE LAST ONES LEFT

C IA Headquarters, Langley
      Okay Gib, it's report card day.

She was back at CIA headquarters, walking through the halls after her first assignment, forever changed. She had been in debriefings all day and was headed to see Caldwell for the first time since Bermuda.

When she arrived at Omicron, the team was gone. In fact, the entire floor was empty. She looked at her watch: 8 p.m.

"Twelve hours of debriefing, fuck me," she said.

She was slightly disappointed none of the team had stuck around. There was no ceremony, no hero's welcome; just another day, and it was over.

She decided she'd face the music and go to Director Caldwell now. He hadn't attended any of her debriefings. She knew he had to be upset. She wanted to clear the air.

When she reached his office, he was there alone at his desk.

What do I say to him?

She had ignored several direct orders and multiple calls. They would fire her, she thought.

She figured she should just break the ice. "Director Caldwell, I just wanted to say that—"

115

"29.96 seconds." Without looking up from his laptop, Director Caldwell replied.

She was confused, not sure what to do with what he'd just said. "Sir, I'm not following you. What does that have to do with—"

"When I use the bathroom, I wash my hands for exactly 29.96 seconds," Caldwell said.

She was even more confused by his clarity.

Caldwell stopped typing and leaned back in his chair. "I'm sure by now you've heard I was our government's asset in Al Qaeda, starting in the late 90s. I was undercover for two years before they trusted me with any significant intel. During that time, I converted to Islam. At first, it was just to work my alias, because I was a Christian. In fact, I was the head deacon at my church. But during that time undercover, I did things in the field no God could forgive. Allah became my light."

Shanice sat in the chair in front of his desk as he continued. "When I moved up the ranks in Al Qaeda, my first assignment was to train the men who would later be responsible for the most horrible terrorist attack on American soil in modern history. I was barely able to communicate stateside.

"For two years, those men were my brothers. We worshiped together, prayed together, ate together, and fought together. I met their children, and they were willing to die for a cause they believed in. Still, I made the call to the CIA that Al Qaeda was going to attack the United States. Saying anything else would've gotten me killed, and my assignment was to find the head of the organization, whom we didn't even know at the time."

Caldwell took off his glasses and rubbed his eyes, then looked at Shanice. "I had to watch 2,996 people die, because I was trying not to blow my cover to get to Osama Bin Laden. I have to live with that. So, every time I use the restroom, I set my timer for 29.96 seconds and I wash my hands for exactly that long, as a reminder that the blood of those innocent people is on my hands."

He turned to the window as Shanice processed his words. As he gazed into the great beyond, she could sense he was no longer talking to her. Maybe he wasn't even talking to himself, but the 2,996 souls lost on that tragic day.

"When I get old, and I can't remember the name of my kids, or what day it is, or even my name, I want to remember to wash my hands for exactly 29.96 seconds. I owe them that much."

There was a pause as he got lost in his memories. After a minute he shook his head and turned back to Shanice. "I was hard on you because that's my job. But this morning, as I stopped for my morning coffee, I went to my local bakery and paid with my usual form of payment before realizing that that was only possible because you did *your* job. No one may ever know it, but the world is still in one piece because of your work, and we have you to thank for that, Agent Zero. Or should I refer to you by your new code name?"

"Wait, so we do give out code names?"

Caldwell nodded, rolling his eyes as Shanice jumped up and pumped her fist in the air. She sat down just as Victor Reynolds, aka Hal, walked into the office.

Shanice said, "Shouldn't you be in a hospital somewhere?"

"Maybe, but where's the fun in that? You giving the kid her code name?" Hal asked as he turned to Caldwell.

"She's earned it."

Shanice smiled from ear to ear as Caldwell continued. "Every agent starts off with code name Zero, and we don't change it until the end of your first mission, because we don't know who's going to make it back – physically or mentally. But you've earned it. So, what's it going to be?"

Shanice bit her fist in excitement and looked at Hal, who shrugged.

She turned back to Caldwell. "I've been imagining this day since I was a kid, but I could never settle on one."

"What does your gut tell you?" Hal wondered.

"I'm thinking Black Goddess."

"I can tell you that one is already taken." Caldwell responded, shocking Shanice.

"Are you serious?"

"I know her personally."

"That was my first choice! Damn it. I refuse to believe y'all hire this many black people." lol

Caldwell and Hal laughed before Caldwell asked, "Well, what's your backup name?

"I didn't have one. How did you come up with Raven Claw?"

Director Caldwell chuckled. "It's a long, uninteresting story. Tell you what, you're on break for a while. Go decompress. Figure out your new normal and get back to me later this week."

"That sounds like a plan."

Shanice got up to leave and gave Hal a fist bump.

Director Caldwell called out from behind her. "One last thing. An interesting article came out of Turks and Caicos today. It featured a myth in West Indian folklore, about a woman who died at sea and became a witch, who was just as deadly to the good and the wicked. They're blaming the death of their prime minister, as well as an attack on a Russian oligarch in the middle of the night, on her. Not to mention the disappearance of an entire villa, and a yacht explosion off the coast of the island. They're calling her Suki.. Soyken... S—"

"Soucouyant," she chimed in.

It was a word she hadn't heard in years, but one that had followed her all her life.

She looked at Hal, who could tell what she was thinking. "I see your wheels turning, kid."

She nodded and looked at the director. "I want that to be my codename."

Caldwell stroked a few keys on his laptop and, after a few moments said, "Done. Welcome to the CIA, Agent Soucouyant."

"Thank you." Didn't even ask how to spell it?

She smiled. She'd been through so much. Learned so much. Come are

Her missions would always be different and challenging, but she knew she was capable, and that Director Caldwell felt the same way.

She shared with him something she'd been holding on to since before she went undercover. "Sir, I don't know if you know this, but you're one of the reasons I wanted to join the CIA. Not as Director Caldwell, but as Raven Claw. As you both know, I lost my parents on 9/11, and it always comforted me to know that someone was out there avenging this horrible wrong.

"I don't know the politics around here, and I don't care. I just know that not every hero dies in uniform. It's an honor, sir. Thank you for your service."

Shanice saluted him. It wasn't CIA tradition, but they both were Army first, and Caldwell understood the sign of respect she was showing him.

He removed his glasses, stood at attention and, looking her squarely in the eyes, saluted her back.

When they were done, Director Caldwell said, "Well, you're officially a ghost now, so disappear."

"I'm out."

She smiled and nodded, walking out of sight.

Director Caldwell leaned on his desk as his grin faded.

"You know, eventually you're gonna have to tell her." Winters,

"Not now, Agent Reynolds."

"She deserves to know."

"And what would you have me say?"

"Not my place, but I do know that if I'd grown up thinking my parents were killed, only to find out they may actually still be alive, I'd want the people who knew that to tell me as much." No way

"Thank you, Agent Reynolds, I appreciate your input." Caldwell continued to type as Hal got up to leave.

He turned around before he reached the door. "Hey, it's not my responsibility, so I won't say anything, but I'll let you in on something you might already know. Sandoval's men weren't just run-of-the-mill street thugs. We're talking ex-KGB, former Delta force, you name it. Twelve highly-trained killers and her in a building, and she's the only one alive to tell the story. That's not even counting the three she killed on the yacht."

"What's your point?"

"My point is, we haven't seen an agent like her in years. I can't take her, and even in your prime, I'm not sure who'd win head-to-head. The kid's a force of nature, and if she ever gets wind of this, heaven help whoever stands in her way."

22
OF DAYS PAST

*S*hanice waited outside the condo. Her mind was racing, still remembering what it felt like to be Mari Patterson.

She'd wept obsessively each time she touched her necklace and thought about the man she'd come to love over the last six months.

There would be no gifts tomorrow, no questions to answer, no cat-and-mouse game of getting to know one another. There would be no thoughtful gestures. There was nothing. Her once-full life had instantly become an empty void and, to make matters worse, she couldn't go back to her old life.

She was a shape-shifting ghost, which is what a Soucouyant was in West Indian culture, so her code name fitted perfectly. But even ghosts have things they can't let go. She was waiting on one of those things.

"There she goes."

Shanice pulled her hoodie over her head and followed the woman who had just parked her car and entered through the gate. Shanice kept her head down and followed her into the building, but didn't get on the elevator; instead she took the stairs up to the second floor. When she entered the hallway, the woman was unlocking her door.

She walked toward the woman who wasn't paying her any attention.

When she was about to open the door, Shanice called her name.

"Tee."

Katrina Carter turned around and her eyes widened in shock.

Shanice quickly walked into the apartment, pulling her inside and locking the door behind them. She wasn't supposed to be there, but she couldn't let her best friend think she was dead. *Breaking Code*

Trina dropped her belongings, still stunned by her friend's presence, and finally said, "You're... I went to your funeral."

"I couldn't tell any—"

Trina slapped Shanice across the face and began to cry.

Shanice embraced her friend as she sobbed.

"Why did you leave me like that?"

"I didn't have a choice. I didn't get a choice from the CIA."

The two hugged and cried.

The pair spent the night catching up on every detail as Trina pulled out an antipasto spread for them to eat.

Shanice felt that she could finally decompress, telling her friend everything that had happened. By midnight, the pair were fully aware of each other's last eight months.

Trina sipped the wine, processing the wild events she'd just heard. "So to recap, you met a brother that looks like a young, British Johnny Gill with dreadlocks, speaks four languages, treated you better than a princess and dicked you down on the regular, all the while taking you around the world on his yacht... and you killed him?"

"He was more like British Tupac with an I.T. degree, and you're leaving out the fact that a terrorist, Trina."

"Okay, girlfriend, you're not helping yourself with that argument. We'll stick with Johnny Gill."

"Whatever."

"In which case, all I can say is: my, my, my. Ha! See what I did there?" Trina hollered, at her reference to Johnny Gill's smash-hit record, My My My.

Those who knew, know, No need to explain a joke

Shanice threw the pillow at her friend before she picked up her glass of chardonnay.

Trina flipped her off while grabbing a piece of cheese as the two embraced their reunion. She'd missed her friend, and she knew she wouldn't be able to see her much after tonight. In fact, life would never be the same. She accepted that.

Still, at this moment, it was good to be home. She needed to unpack the last nearly eight months of her life with the only person she could do that with: her best friend, Katrina Carter. She watched her friend, who was already tipsy, as she took a sip of the wine.

"See, that's the problem right there. Bitches like you."

"Me? I'm sorry. All I did was save the world."

"But in the process, did you have to throw a good black man away?"

"He was going to set the world back to the stone ages!"

"See, sis, I swear to god you don't be thinking."

"What are you say—"

"I'm about to tell you." Trina said, clapping her hands.

Shanice took a large gulp of wine, because she knew her friend was about to become even more animated. Trina continued to clap her hands a few more times.

"Shan Shan, let me tell you one thing for certain, and two things for sho': if that was me trying to save the world from a sexy, dark chocolate deluxe, good-smelling, fine-ass man catering to my every need, he could set this motherfucker back to the Fred Flintstone ages for all I care. As long as when he's done blowing up the world, he comes and blows out this back... on a yacht, of course."

"I should throw this glass at you."

The pair chuckled at Trina's half-joking nature.

Her words stung because she was still heavily conflicted about the assignment. She missed Sandoval. His smile, his passion, his questions. She loved him, and was too afraid to admit it, because it meant she'd failed at the one thing she wanted more than anything: being a CIA asset.

She thought back to the first day she met Caldwell and their conversation.

If the kind of moral ambiguity of letting your childhood friend die knowing you could have saved his life bothers you, then this is definitely not a job you should take.

It made sense now. There were no good answers, just problems that needed solutions, and it was her job to live with the burden. It was her responsibility as a CIA agent – as Agent Soucouyant.

She turned back to her friend, who was still rambling about what she'd be doing in her shoes. "You'd have to eventually live on that yacht because every country on Earth would break down. It would literally be a war zone."

"Water doesn't scare me. Hell, 70 percent of the world is made up of water. I'm trying to ride that London tower... what's it called?"

"Trina."

"Oh yeah, Big Ben."

"Girl, if you don't—"

"I'm just saying, give the brother a chance to fix his ways."

"Trina, he was planning to devastate the entire world's economy. You know that Range Rover you love so much? How you gonna drive that with no money?"

"Yeah, but I wouldn't have these student loans either. If I had to lose driving a Range to not pay Sallie Mae, believe me, I'd be walking. But it wouldn't matter because I'd be on my yacht trying to make that London bridge fall down. Hey!" She lifted her hands in the air and mimicked the sexual act of being on top.

Shanice threw another pillow at her friend. "Is that all you think about? Dick?"

"Honey, I know you like doing push-ups and eating food from cans, but speaking for the rest of us sensible and normal women, I want my bills paid, and my back rubbed or broken, and not in that particular order."

"I just don't want you to lose sight of the fact that the man was trying to destroy the planet."

"Uh, have you seen Earth lately? This place could use some fixing up. As long as he fixed me when he was done, I don't care what he did. I'm good. I'm trying to get these eggs… white. Ha! You see what I did there?" She laughed as she rubbed her stomach.

Shanice rolled her eyes. "God must've run out of sense when he made you. The man slaughtered an island full of groundskeepers and maids."

"Okay, now that was foul… Lord, why does good dick have to be so problematic?" she asked half-jokingly as Shanice sipped the red chardonnay they'd been nursing. *lol*

"I think in another life I could've been with Sandoval. There was a moment when we were facing each other. He had a gun to someone's head, and he asked me if I loved him the way he loved me, and for a second, I wavered. Maybe he was telling the truth. Maybe he was coming back to get me, and we'd spend our days sailing from port to port."

"Would you have gone with him?"

"It doesn't matter now, but I guess a part of me wants to know it was real. I mean, outside of trying to bring about the end of days, he was everything I wanted in a man."

"So, what are you going to do now?"

"I have a break before I go back out in the field. They want me to decompress. But I'm going to take care of some business."

Katrina poured another glass for the two of them. "Oh, let me guess. Go see Marcus' bobblehead ass. Talking about problematic dick."

"Trina!"

"You need to let it go."

"Elaine tried to kill me, Tee, and she's killing Marcus."

Trina put her glass down and shook her head as she rubbed her temples. "Black Jesus, I can't today, Lord."

"I gotta tell him the truth about his condition."

"You know him and Becky with the red hair got married, right?"

"Wait, he… What?" *and he supposed to be dead by now.*

The words shocked Shanice. *you been gone 8 months now*

Trina pulled up his social profile to show him and Elaine holding hands.

Shanice grabbed the phone as a wave of emotions filled her.

Trina took a sip of her wine. "That's right, while you were out here saving the world from Idris Elba's fine little brother, Marcus told old Becky she was the cream to his coffee."

Shanice was a ball of confusion. She still hadn't resolved her feelings for Sandoval, and she wasn't yet ready to deal with her feelings for Marcus, but she did have a score to settle with Elaine.

It was a lot to deal with, and nothing she felt like diving into while reuniting with her best friend. Still, she knew her friend needed to hear a response in order for things to feel normal. She turned to Trina. "Doesn't matter. Elaine tried to kill me, and I'm going to put a bullet in her."

"Whoa, sis, hold on."

"What, Tee?"

"You can't just be in here planning homicides like you picking out earrings. You not gonna have them folk run up in my house while you're in Madagascar fighting crimes." Trina raised her voice to no one in particular. "Um, excuse me, Detective Stabler and Benson, if you're listening, I had nothing to do with this."

"I'm in the CIA, Trina. I can literally kill just about anyone."

"Wait... they give you an actual license to kill?"

"I've been killing people since I was nineteen. When you get to this level, they don't have to, but for the record, yes, they do. It's actually a physical card we have to carry."

"For real?"

"No. Not in the least. Why would they give you a card? I can't believe you're stupid enough to fall for that." Shanice joked as she pointed at her friend, who flipped her off.

"Fuck you, Shan Shan," Trina said as she hit Shanice with a throw pillow.

Shanice continued to tease her. "I'm just saying, I don't understand how they let you work on brains when you ain't got none." lol

"Do not talk to me about having no brains when you gave up a man willing to rebuild the world in your image for... Marcus."

Trina pretended to gag as Shanice flipped her off. "What the fuck ever. I said what I said."

"Girl, if I could fight, I'd be whooping your ass right now. Now we can play all you want, but make no mistake: I'm a damn good surgeon, I have to be to fix this trainwreck of a love life you have."

"Whatever."

"Yeah, whatever." The two were quiet for a second before Trina asked, "Wait, just so we're clear: I'm not sworn to secrecy or nothing, am I?"

"Yeah, you are. This is pretty much as secret as it gets."

"But Shan, I thou—"

"I'm supposed to be dead, Trina, and just about everything I told you is top-level security clearance information. If you reveal it on a recorded phone line or in person, there's a good chance the CIA or some other government organization will find you and hold you hostage. Worst-case scenario, you and everyone you love could get killed. If I were you, I'd keep our little chat to myself."

Shanice watched her friend, now mortified by the burden. Shanice sipped more of the wine. "Quit acting like you just found out Batman is Bruce Wayne. You just gotta treat this with the same confidentiality as you would a medical patient of yours."

"No, it's not that, it's just… you know I don't have a lot of friends, Shan Shan. When I thought you were dead, I said to myself, 'okay, she'd want you to be strong, she'd want you to keep pushing', and so I did. I put one foot in front of the other, trying to deal with the fact that my ace was gone. Trina took a sip of wine and continued.

"For you to come back, only to never know if you're gonna be back again…" A tear welled in Trina's eye. Shanice scooted over on the couch and hugged her friend tightly as Trina let her emotions flow.

After a moment, Shanice spoke. "We'll make it work, Tee. I promise." She wiped the tear from Trina's face as the two held on to each other for a bit longer.

Shanice didn't know when she'd see her friend again, but she knew it was time to pay a visit to her other best friend. Her next stop was Houston, Texas.

NO MORE QUESTIONS, JUST ANSWERS

THE ANSWERS BEGIN IN SEDUCTION II

followed by Money Power & Sex II
coming soon.

- ○ Ronnie
- ○ Seduction 2
- ○ MPS 2
- ○ In the case of Alexandia Hughes
  └ Detective who put Donovan away

ABOUT THE AUTHOR

Norian Love is an emerging author of sci-fi thrillers. This is Norian's seventeenth book.

ALSO BY NORIAN LOVE

Director Caldwell (malik)   ½ Black, half Arabic   P 2
aka Raven Claw   6-1   light brown eyes
P1 President ignored 9/11 threat

Xavier Digs. Professor + cybersecurity p2
likes cars + boats, like her p10

"Hal" aka Agent Victor Reynolds — held her hostage in the
cabin   shot him in the leg

p3 The Seven Syndicate   Leader Sandoval — Latin man?   aka Adams Carter
                          dark skinned, dred locks, British accent

Shanice 5-7   p2   " Agent Zero "
                p3   Code names are earned in the field
1st assignment : "Starkiss" hacker

P117 wanted code name "Black Goddess"   1st choice
  P118 Souccwynd

Made in United States
North Haven, CT
25 February 2023

33184049R00078